JENNA TESTS THE WATERS

Summer Lifeguards

ELIZABETH DOYLE CAREY

sourcebooks
young readers

Published by Sourcebooks Young Readers, an imprint of Sourcebooks Kids
P.O. Box 4410, Naperville, Illinois 60567-4410
(630) 961-3900
sourcebookskids.com

Originally published as *Junior Lifeguards: The Test* in 2017 in
the United States of America by Dunemere Books.

Library of Congress Cataloging-in-Publication data is on file with the publisher.

Source of Production: Versa Press, East Peoria, Illinois, United States
Date of Production: March 2021
Run Number: 5021070

Printed and bound in the United States of America.
VP 10 9 8 7 6 5 4 3 2 1

Summer
LIFEGUARDS

THE SUMMER LIFEGUARDS SERIES

For the #brave and #strong Hammam sisters

1

A Bright Idea

All I ever wanted was to be an Olympic swimmer. Glory, honor, excellence, patriotism—it all appealed to me. I always pictured myself up there on the top step of the podium in my Ralph Lauren–designed team warm-up suit—red, white, and blue, of course—waving at the crowd, bowing my head for the gold medal, receiving my flowers, and wiping away a modest tear as *The Star-Spangled Banner* played over the sound system for all to hear. The crowd is cheering for me: responsible, reliable, hardworking Jenna

Bowers, from Westham, Massachusetts, as I win the world's highest athletic honor.

More than anything, more even than winning, I love to swim—the relaxation of the pace and rhythm, the feeling of power as I slice through the water. It's hypnotizing and it takes me outside myself for a while, and then it brings me back to earth with a post-workout euphoria. It's what I'm good at, and that skill defines me.

But over the years, my joy in swimming has been replaced by times and stats and schedules, endless meets and practices, unglamorous travel and early mornings, jockeying for position on my own team, and monitoring my standing in my league. If this is all there is, then my Olympic dreams are wavering.

I swim at the Y here in Westham on Cape Cod, where I've been on the team for the past five years. I'd like to say I'm the star of the team, because I was for a really long time. But about six months ago, some new girls joined up, and either they were better or I got worse, and now I'm number three or maybe two on a really good day.

At first, this stunk. I hated being seeded third and watching my coach fall all over these two girls the way she'd once fallen all over me. (I think once my coach realized she wasn't going to be an Olympic swimmer herself, she decided the next best thing would be to "discover" and coach an Olympic swimmer.) It had been fun being the star. But then it started to bother me that when I'd lose, which was rare, everyone would want to pick apart why I'd lost: my coach, my teammates, my parents, and even my brothers! They'd say my breathing was off or my flip turn was too open or I'd been slow off the block. I wanted to say to them all: "Fine! Then you get in the pool, and let's see how you do it!"

And when I started losing more (not badly, by the way—just not winning all the time, like usual), there was more criticism and more hard training, and right then the new girls showed up and, well...after a while, it was kind of fun watching someone else get ripped to shreds after a bad race, and seeing someone else do twenty extra laps for a change. The heat was off, and I felt a lot cooler.

Right about then, maybe a month ago, I saw the first flyer.

It said: "Be a hero! Learn to save lives! Westham Junior Lifeguards tryout info coming soon!" and it gave the website for the town lifeguarding program so you could learn more.

But, most importantly, it was being tacked up on the bulletin board at the YMCA by a really cute high school guy named Luke Slater (not that I actually knew him; I just knew who he was). Physically, he wasn't my type. He was kind of short, and I am tall. He was a little too old for me, and he had white blond hair, while I like guys with dark hair, but his big green eyes were friendly as he called out, "Come on out for tryouts! We're going to post the official date in the next couple of weeks, okay?" And then he grinned at me, so I had to smile back.

"Okay!" I replied, because what else could I say?

I'd heard about kids at school who trained to be Junior Lifeguards; they were always kids I admired but didn't really have time to hang out with because of swimming. When I was younger, we had a babysitter named Molly who did the training every summer and then became an ocean guard. She was so nice and pretty and cool, and on the rare summer weekends when I didn't have a swim meet, I'd head to Lookout Beach for an afternoon where I'd see her at work. She'd sit up high on the lifeguard stand in her red Speedo one-piece and tight ponytail, a whistle around her neck and zinc on her nose. It was like she was the boss of the beach. She'd tell kids what they were and weren't allowed to do and blow her whistle and everyone would obey her. But she'd always wave at me and ask about swim team and how my brothers were. It was like being friends with a celebrity; I was psyched when people would see her talking to me from way up high on her lifeguard throne.

At the end of her shift, the boy lifeguards would often tease her and throw her in the water—everyone would laugh and yell. It looked like so much fun! Like a movie of what being a teenager should be like. Handsome boys joking around with pretty girls in the sunshine at the water's edge, and getting paid for it too! I hadn't seen her much since she'd left for college three years ago, but whenever I thought of lifeguards, I thought of Molly Cruise.

For a while, I'd forgotten about Junior Lifeguards. Then today, a Monday, everything changed. Today's swim practice at the Y started off like any other: I biked over from school, changed into my suit in the locker room, stashed my stuff, and grabbed my goggles and towel. But on my way out to the pool room, I saw a new flyer—a big poster, really.

JUNIOR LIFEGUARD TRYOUTS
THIS SATURDAY!
10:00 a.m. at the Westham YMCA pool.

Visit our website for forms and details at www.juniorguards.com.

Daily practices
M–F 1:00–5:00 p.m.
Weekend tournaments.

I felt a little butterfly in my stomach flutter around, but I pushed it away. I had a swim meet up the Cape this weekend, so there was no way I could attend the tryout. Too bad.

In the pool room that day, we had our team meeting on the bleachers, then everyone warmed up and jumped in the water. We worked on our weakest stroke first, and I couldn't stop thinking of the lifeguard tryout as I did the breaststroke up and down the pool. I wondered whether the test would be on certain strokes, or if it would be more about endurance. I'm in really good shape (not to brag), so I knew I could ace an endurance test. If I had to pick a stroke, I'd probably pick butterfly. I bet that would stand out, since most people can't do it.

"Let's go, Bowers! Head out of the clouds, please!" Coach Randall called as she strolled past my lane. How could she tell what I was thinking? I tried harder for a few laps, my head empty of everything but the rhythm: pull, pull, kick, breathe; pull, pull, kick, breathe; pull, pull, kick, breathe. I usually sing a song in my head to keep my rhythm going, but today I had been distracted, so there was no musical accompaniment. Quickly, I started singing the newest Taylor Swift song in my head, and it got me back on track. But then, during a water break, I heard two of the new girls discussing the lifeguard tryouts poster, and I got all distracted again.

"It would be hilarious to watch all those kids splashing around in here, wouldn't it?" said one of them.

The other laughed. "I've heard a couple have to be saved themselves every year!"

"Amateurs!" the first girl laughed.

They were nice girls, but smug and overly secure in their little swim-team world. For some reason, it rubbed me the wrong way today. I thought of Molly and those handsome boy lifeguards. There was nothing amateur about them. If anything, they seemed like professionals, almost adults, to me. Being a lifeguard took nerve! If someone was in trouble in the water, you had to go in and save them, no matter what! Bad weather, sharks, huge waves...anything! It was hard core, like the marines.

Practice was almost over, and it was time for a final time trial, all in, best strokes all around.

Bweeet!

Coach Randall blew her whistle, and we were off! I dove in with hardly a splash, then cut through the water and porpoised as far as I could before surfacing for a stroke and a breath. As I said, butterfly is my best stroke, and I've been working for months to shave a few seconds off my time. Every second counted these days.

My wet hand slapped the concrete end of the pool and Coach Randall was there, as always. She clicked her stopwatch and nodded. "Thirty-two seconds. Not your best, Bowers," and then she moved down the lanes. I could see that the two other girls in my heat had beaten me—the ones who'd been talking about the Junior Lifeguard tryouts.

I sighed heavily and snapped my goggles off my eyes so I could massage the dents they'd left in my skin. Slowly, I hoisted myself up and out to change. As I walked to the locker room, I passed the tryouts poster again and felt the butterflies, though this time, there were more of them.

After I showered, changed, pinned up my shoulder-length hair (which used to be blond but is currently light greenish from chlorine), dropped some eye drops into my dark brown eyes, and put on my hoodie, flip-flops, and a layer of bubblegum lip gloss, I slammed my locker shut, grabbed my backpack, and went to unlock my bike and ride home. But just as I cut across the lobby of the Y, I heard Coach Randall calling me from her office.

I turned and saw her at her desk, waving me in. "Hey, Coach," I called. I suddenly felt nervous, but I wasn't sure why.

"Jenna, come on in and take a seat."

Uh-oh, I thought. Coach Randall never calls me by my first name.

"Is something wrong?" I asked, lowering myself onto the chair next to the desk in her cramped office. My mouth was dry, and my heart was thudding. Could she know that I had been fantasizing about Junior Lifeguards?

Coach Randall looked at me kindly. "You seemed a little distracted in there today. Are you okay?" she asked.

Her kindness caught me off guard. We don't really talk about feelings on swim team.

"Oh... I..." I could feel a blush blooming on my cheeks.

"I know things have gotten more competitive around here, but you've always been my star! I just haven't seen your usual effort lately. We have a lot of big meets coming up, and I just wanted to make sure your heart is in it and that nothing's bothering you, on swim team or otherwise." She studied me with her head tipped to the side.

I sighed. It was weird, but it was like something inside me just broke open. I felt my eyes welling up with tears. Coach Randall reached out and put her hand on mine.

"Oh, Jenna! I'm sorry! I didn't mean to make you cry!" With her other hand, she reached for some tissues and handed it to me as I snuffled awkwardly.

"Thanks. I was thinking... It's not about swim team. I do enjoy swim team. I just I thought it might be fun to... I don't know. This is going to sound really bad..."

"Go ahead. It's okay," encouraged Coach Randall.

I took a deep breath and dashed the tears from my eyes. I smiled shakily. "I thought it would be fun to try out for Junior Lifeguards. Absurd, I know! I really don't have time for that. It was just a thought. I'm over it already."

Coach Randall smiled gently and sat back in her seat, folding her arms across her chest. "Is this a sudden thought or something that's been on your mind for a while?"

I sighed. "Ever since I saw the first poster. I guess a few weeks. It just looked like fun, you know?"

Coach Randall sighed too. "I know. It is fun. I did it when I was your age."

"Really?" I asked. I was surprised. It was hard to picture Coach Randall on the beach.

She nodded and swiveled her chair, looking up at the ceiling thoughtfully. "You know, I think a lot about how hard we push you kids these days. Things have become so professional, so competitive. You don't have any free time like we used to when I was your age. It's always on to the next meet, or practice, or test."

I nodded. "I'm used to it, though. I can handle it." I sat up straight. *Brilliant, Bowers*, I scolded myself. *Crying in*

front of your coach about how swim team is no fun! That's a
great way to keep a top spot on the team.

Coach Randall leaned forward again and looked at me carefully. "How about if we make a deal?" she said, squinting.

"What?" I could just imagine where this was heading: extra practices, weight training, more meets...

"How would you like to take the summer off and train with the Junior Lifeguards instead of the swim team? I'll save your spot for you, and you can join back up in the fall. What would you think about that?" She folded her arms again and watched me.

I couldn't help it. A huge smile bloomed on my face. "Wait, *really*? Are you joking?" I looked around the room. "Am I being punked? Is this a trick?"

Coach Randall laughed. "No. It's not a trick. Think of it as cross-training. I think it might renew your interest in swim team if you can get out in the world and see how good your skills are compared to everyone else's. I had the chance to do it when I was a kid, so why shouldn't you?"

"But losing three months of training...and competition. I'll fall so far behind!"

"Tell you what. You can come to practice whenever you like, but we'll say at least once a week. That way you can keep a hand in, and you won't fall out of touch with what's going on. I see your interest level wobbling a bit, and I'd hate to lose you from the team. You've got a ton of talent, and both of us have put a lot of work into your skill development, not to mention your parents and all their time and energy. It would be a shame for all of us if you quit, and it would be a waste for you to stay here when your heart's not in it. If you go on a break starting today, I'll just bet you that you'll come back refreshed and raring to go in September. What do you say?"

I couldn't help myself. I laughed and jumped up and hugged Coach Randall. "Thank you so much!" I cried. "This is awesome! I can't wait to tell my parents!"

She laughed too, and hugged me back. "I'd maybe pose it as a question to them first, if I were you. See what they say and have them give me a call so we can discuss it. I think... I think it's the right thing to do, Jenna. You'll see."

"Thanks, Coach."

"You'll make a great lifeguard, kid!" she said.

"I bet you were great at it too!" I said.

Coach Randall laughed. "Nah. I was terrible. I only wanted to watch the gorgeous guys!"

"Well, sometimes they need saving too!" I joked. I stood in her doorway as I was leaving. "Thanks, Coach. This is... This is like a gift. I really appreciate it."

She nodded. "I'm glad we could work something out. Go get 'em!"

I practically skipped to my bike I was so happy. I couldn't believe how things had turned around in such a short amount of time. I'd gone from a normal day of school and swim team, to suddenly heading into a new

adventure, with a summer doing just what I wanted to do!
How lucky was I?

All I knew was that I needed to talk to my best friend,
Piper, as soon as humanly possible. And I knew just what
I needed to talk to her about: Junior Lifeguards. The nervous butterflies flapped wildly around in my stomach as I
raced to her farm on my bike. And this time, I didn't push
them away. I was getting used to them. They felt kind of
good, actually. They'd feel even better if Piper agreed to
do Junior Lifeguards with me, but that was going to be a
challenge.

Unemployed

Piper's family, the Janssenses, and my family, the Bowerses, go way back in Westham. Like, generations and generations. Westham and the surrounding area used to be populated by just farmers and fishermen in the olden days, and we always had "summer people," but they were low-key. However, in recent years, it has become popular with much wealthier summer people than we were used to, which has changed things. Farms have been gobbled up and changed into luxury golf courses, formerly public areas (like beach access and fishing ponds) have become private—with signs and fences to keep out strangers—and things are a lot more crowded.

The crowds are great for local-business-owning families like mine (fishing boat captains, farm-stand operators, painting contractors) and Piper's (they own a riding stable), but not so great for traffic, house prices, mom-and-pop stores in town, and stuff like that. It's also not great for kids who don't have rich parents, like us, because things like the movies and bowling are so expensive. Plus, Piper's parents are divorced, and they both had to move far away for their jobs, at least for a while. Piper didn't want to move to Ohio or Pennsylvania, so her grandmother, Bett, offered to keep her here, which worked out great for everyone. But Piper doesn't like asking Bett for pocket money, and her parents aren't able to send her much.

Piper and I know that when summer comes, it's time to make money. Our families in Westham work like crazy from Memorial Day to Labor Day to make every penny they can, because things really drop off after that. If they don't kill it in the summer, things get pretty lean in Cape Cod by February or March. Piper and I are used to it, and we pitch in and work hard too; I work at my mom's family's farm stand, and Piper works at her grandma Bett's barn. Our jobs pay decently (the tips are what really count), so it's worth it, and it would be hard to give up, unless something really great came along.

I thought about all of this as I stand-up pedaled all the way to the Janssenses' barn. I couldn't get there fast enough.

"Piper!" I called, dropping my bike in the dirt outside the main barn door. My legs were shaking, but I couldn't tell if it was from my news or all of that hard bike riding. I stumbled across the dirt barnyard.

"In here!" she replied.

I'd held it together the whole ride and now, just hearing Piper's voice, I wanted to burst. I entered the dim barn, my eyes blinking to adjust and my nose twitching.

Four-thirty was muck-out time. So, it was dusty and fragrant in there. The new hay smelled sweet but the old hay, well...yuck.

"Where?" I called again, urgent to see her.

"With Buttercup!" she replied and poked her head out of a stall halfway down the row. She narrowed her eyes and leaned on her pitchfork, her two long braids the same buttery color as the bales of hay all around. "What's up?" she asked kindly. "You sound funny."

"OMG, you are never going to believe this!" I squealed. "Coach Randall has given me a leave of absence from swim team!" And then I sank down on a hay bale as the reality sank in, and my legs gave out from the flat-out pedaling to the Janssenses'.

Piper crossed the barn in three quick strides and was at my side, plopping down next to me on the hay. "Wait, *what*? Are you sure? Swim team is your life!"

"Of course I'm sure!" I cried. "And it's not my life anymore. It's time for a new life!" I declared. I sat up straight, took a deep breath, and said, "It's time for some adventure!"

"Okay, whoa! Back up, girl. Tell me what happened." Piper sat back against a rough plank wall, her hands on her dirty tan jodhpurs and her head tilted patiently.

I rolled my eyes a little because I hate it when Piper talks to me like I'm a horse, but I didn't want to get in a fight about it right now when I needed her. I explained about Coach Randall and Junior Lifeguards, and Piper listened in amazement.

At the end, she said, "But are you sure you want to quit? I mean, it was kind of a spontaneous decision, right? What are your parents going to say?"

But I shook my head. "I'm not quitting! That's the beauty of it. I can try something new, *and* I can go back when I'm done! I'll go to one practice a week. Plus, I think Junior Lifeguards will be awesome, don't you?" I couldn't ask her point-blank to do it with me because it would scare her off. This was going to have to be handled just right.

Piper is a very strong athlete who does not particularly enjoy swimming, though she is good at it. I was going to have to work on that in order to convince her to try out with me.

Piper sighed heavily. "So, wait. Junior Lifeguards? Seriously? How will you make money? When will you go to swim team practice?"

I nodded. I'd already thought of this. "I'll do the morning shift at the farm stand, weekdays only. On Fridays, I can make the swim team practice because it's late. Then Junior Lifeguards is on afternoons and weekends."

"You won't make as much money working weekday mornings at the farm stand," she pointed out, picking a scrap of hay off her starched white polo shirt. I usually work on weekends when I can make some big tips carrying out bags to the summer people's cars.

I sighed. "No."

As much as I like making money, Piper lives for it. Ever since her parents left, Piper has worked for her grandma Bett every chance she got, teaching pony camp, currying the horses that the rich kids board there, mucking out stalls, and more. She's already socked away more than two thousand dollars.

I pressed my case. "It's not all about the money, Pipe. I want to have fun too. I want to maybe hang out with boys and have a social life. And I think Junior Lifeguards will look good on my college applications one day too. Especially, if I'm not the swim team hotshot I used to be."

"Jenna!" scolded Piper. "Don't think like a quitter."

"I'm thinking like a realist," I said. "A realist who one day could be pulling down eighteen bucks an hour as a Westham Ocean Beach Lifeguard!"

"That's a long way off!" laughed Piper.

"You gotta start somewhere!" I said with a shrug. "You'd be good at it too," I added quietly.

"Ha!" laughed Piper with a short, dry bark.

Hmm. I could see that I should have spun this differently. Piper is *obsessed* with boys. I should have led with the boy angle!

"Come on, Piper," I said. "There will be so many boys…"

Piper rolled her eyes. "You are not talking me into this like you do with everything else. Not this time, sister!"

I backed off.

We both sighed, and suddenly, the notes of a familiar whistle carried into the barn on the late May breeze.

"Bett," said Piper.

Piper's grandmother, Bett Janssens, is a dynamo. When Piper's grandfather died twenty years ago, Bett took over the family stables and turned it into the number one riding establishment in our area, which is saying a lot. People of all ages and all abilities flocked to the barn to learn to ride and to have their horses cared for in a "concierge" fashion. Bett's barn was all about service and catering to its wealthy clientele. It helps that it is physically picture perfect, like a Cape Cod postcard: beautifully weathered gray shingled buildings with white trim and shutters; neat gates and fences covered in pale pink rambling roses; and all surrounded by rings and jumps set in endless white-fenced fields that tapered down to the dunes for amazing access to trail riding in the waves. The land alone is worth more than you could ever imagine. Not that Bett would ever sell.

Bett is in great shape and always on the move; the air feels electric when she's around and people treat her very reverently, like she's famous. But as inspiring and impressive as the Bett show can be, it can also be tiring. Bett can make lesser mortals feel like losers very easily. Piper and I took a deep breath and steeled ourselves for the arrival of the whirlwind.

"Girls! Why so serious? It's almost summer!" said Bett cheerfully as three mutts trotted along behind her into the barn. "Lots of peace and quiet and free time to look forward to." She cackled at her own joke and smoothed back her chin-length white hair with one hand as she lifted a brown velvet riding helmet onto her head with the other.

"Are you going to tell?" Piper asked me quietly.

I shrugged. "I guess. I haven't even told my parents yet."

Bett's smile disappeared as she tugged her helmet on

tightly and clipped the clasp under her chin. "What's up, girls?" she asked, smoothly squatting down to hay bale level to meet our eyes. Besides all the riding, Bett is a regular at 6:00 a.m. beach yoga every day.

"I'm taking a sabbatical from swim team," I said, a big smile growing on my face.

"Oh, honey, no kidding! Why?" Bett's blue eyes were full of concern. Despite my smile, she knows very well how much time I spend in the pool at the Y since she's always dropping me there or picking me up on the way to and from my activities with Piper. She reached out and gave me a rough rub on the leg, like I was a newborn colt she needed to warm up.

"I..." I was about to tell her about Junior Lifeguards, but Piper silenced me with a look.

"It's a long story," said Piper.

Bett bit her lip thoughtfully for a minute. "What are you going to do with yourself this summer?" she asked. Idleness would not occur to Bett.

I took a deep breath and made my first formal

announcement on the subject. "Actually, I'm going to try out for Junior Lifeguards," I said, and I smiled. *Take that, Piper!*

Bett raised her eyebrows and smiled back. She looked relieved that I had a plan. "Well, *that's* a wonderful idea!" She said, standing up and giving me a strong clap on the back. "You'll be terrific at that!"

"Thanks." Her confidence strengthened my resolve.

"Maybe Piper should do it with you!" said Bett lightly, but her eyes were serious. She began pulling tackle down from the wall to harness up her giant Arabian workhorse, Layla.

"Ha!" laughed Piper, her blue eyes dancing. "A landlubber like me! Can you imagine?"

"You'd be great at it," said Bett, dead seriously. She slung the tackle over her arm.

Piper's smile faded. "Come on! Hello? It's me, Piper Janssens, you're talking about! Why would *I* do such a thing?"

But I wasn't going to let this opportunity slip by. I

turned to grin encouragingly at Piper. "A change of pace? Social prestige? Get out and see the world a little? Make more money down the road? And we'd have so much fun, Piper! Do it with me!"

Piper rolled her eyes. "Yeah, right. And what would they do without me here?"

Hmmm. That was another challenge for me. Piper liked working at the barn. She wasn't obsessed with caring for horses or riding, though she was good at both. She liked the money, and also, I think, the security of staying home all the time.

"Actually, honey," Bett interrupted, untangling a stubborn lead. She glanced over at me as if deciding whether or not to say what she wanted to say.

Piper turned to look at her. "What?"

"I don't know if this is the right time..." Bett paused.

Piper looked at me then back at her grandmother.

"You can say anything you want in front of Jenna. It's okay." She shrugged. I shrugged too.

"Well…" Bett took a deep breath. "I'm just going to put this out there." She transferred the tackle from one arm to the other and leaned against the side of the barn doorway. "Piper, your parents and I think you need a break from the barn this summer. You need to be out doing other things with your friends, kids your own age—having fun, broadening your horizons, learning new skills."

"What are you talking about?" Piper was confused.

Suddenly, I wished I were anywhere else on earth.

Bett drew a deep breath. "You have the whole rest of your life to work here, not that you have to. We'd just like to see you do something else for a change. I was going to let you know this weekend, but now… Well, maybe you should do Junior Lifeguards with Jenna instead this summer. Since you won't be at the barn, I mean."

"Wait, *what*?" Now Piper was furious, and I think mortified too. She didn't know which way to look or what to say. She spluttered, "Are you saying I'm *fired*?"

"No, dear, I wouldn't fire you," said Bett calmly, though

there was pain in her eyes as she spoke. "I'm simply putting you on a much-needed leave of absence."

Now Piper was becoming teary eyed. "But who will
help out here? And what about the money? I need a job!
Why is it your decision and not mine?"

Bett drew herself up straight and planted her feet in
their boots in a wide stance. (*Uh-oh*, I thought.) "It's for
your own good, Piper. Trust me. And we can work out an
allowance, that's not a problem. You just need a change of
scenery. Something age-appropriate."

Piper was furious. "No way. No *way* am I leaving the
barn! It's not up to you! It's *my* life!" And then she stormed
out, leaving Bett and me staring at each other.

"I think she's a little upset," I said tentatively.

"A little?" Bett managed a small wry smile.

"I'll go after her," I offered.

"Thanks, honey. Better you than me right now, I
think." And Bett turned on her heel and strode down the
alley to Layla's stall.

32

"Let's go, butterflies," I muttered to myself as I followed Piper down the path to the farmhouse.

3

all In

Piper flopped miserably on her bed as I opened up the
Westham Junior Lifeguards homepage on her computer
and read her everything that the lifeguard training program would feature. Every day there would be fitness
activities (not a plus for her, but good for me since I'll
need to stay in good condition if I'm not doing swim
team regularly) and then a new skill or technique would
be introduced. Over the summer, we'd learn CPR, the
Heimlich maneuver, mouth-to-mouth resuscitation,

and other basic first aid skills from the local Emergency Medical Technicians squad. We'd have experts from Woods Hole Oceanographic Institute come tell us about wave patterns, hurricanes, riptides, coastal erosion, lightning, and more. Seasoned local lifeguards would teach us lifesaving techniques like saves and holds, scanning techniques to spot trouble before it's too late, and how to use gear such as life preservers, rescue kayaks and surfboards, and maybe even Jet Skis. There would also be training for lifeguarding competitions, mostly up and down the Cape. (One year, the squad had gone to nationals and won!) And then there was a section on mental preparation, taught by Bud Slater, who must be Luke's dad. He would train us to focus our attention, practice mindfulness, and even meditate.

I read it all out loud to Piper, and she sighed and scoffed and made lots of discouraging noises, but I didn't let it get to me. The only question she asked was, "What do they make you do to try out?" but the website didn't address the specifics, other than that there would be pool and ocean tests this weekend. For the first portion—the pool swim test at the Y on Saturday—we needed to register in advance at the town lifeguarding headquarters at Lookout Beach. We'd have to create an account online for both of us in order to print out an application, then we needed to fill it in, have a waiver signed by our guardians, and pay a fifty-dollar tryout fee. If we passed the pool test, we'd be invited to the ocean test on Sunday at Lookout Beach. If we made it, the program was free.

I busied myself printing out two copies of the program overview, the waiver, and application, while Piper moaned about how she hates swimming, hates wearing a bathing suit in public, doesn't want to waste her time away from the barn, needs to make money, already knows CPR, and so on.

I separated the forms into two stacks and shook them neatly into two small, even piles. "Pipe, here's the pile for you and Bett to fill out. I'll take mine home with me. Let's plan to go after school tomorrow and hand them in at the beach office, okay?"

"I'm not doing it," said Piper, staring up at the ceiling.

I sighed. "Well, at least try out. Then, if you don't pass, you can tell Bett you tried, and maybe she'll let you have your job back. Okay?"

"Humph," said Piper.

I stood up. It was five thirty, and my parents would be home soon and wondering where I was. "Listen, Piper Janssens. We need to have a fun and exciting summer. We're only thirteen once, and Junior Lifeguards is the way to go. It's something new and different for both of us, and it will be interesting. We'll be outside, we'll learn a ton, and down the road, we can be lifeguards together and make good money, and it will help us get into good colleges. If you can think of a better plan for our summer, and for future summers, just let me know!" I was about to leave when I knew it was time to play my ace. "And by the way, it says on the website that certified pool guards make fifteen dollars an hour, and ocean guards can make up to thirty dollars an hour around here."

Piper was silent at first as I flounced out of the room.

Then, "Whatever, traitor!" she called after me.

I grinned. If she was name-calling, it meant I was getting to her.

⟨ornament⟩

After dinner that night, I broke the news to my parents and asked them to fill out the Junior Lifeguard forms for me. Neither of them had the reaction I was hoping for: my dad was annoyed, and my mom was surprised. It was true what Coach Randall had warned me about—we'd all put time into this swimming career of mine, and it wasn't easy for my parents to back away from it. The paperwork sat on the kitchen table, untouched.

"You're going to fall behind, Jen. If you want to get a college scholarship for swimming someday, you can't afford to take a season off." My dad's mouth was set in a grim line.

Having grown up in Westham, my parents are big advocates of "getting out." Even though they both moved back here after college to work in family businesses, they say they have bigger dreams for my three younger brothers and me. Part of that dream is a good education and exposure to the bigger world. Swimming was always going to be my ticket off the Cape.

"I'd hate to see you lose everything you've worked toward," said my mom.

My twelve-year-old brother, Nate, was eavesdropping as he pulled some computer paper from my mom's desk drawer and inserted it into the tray of our family printer. "I think the coach just wants to get rid of you," Nate said snarkily.

I stuck my tongue out at him and waited for my parents to chastise him, but they didn't. They just looked at me.

"Wait, do you think that too?" I asked in shock. "I

just need to talk to Amy Randall in the morning," said my mom wearily. "I'm not sure what I think." She rubbed her eyes.

"Look, I'm all for having a fun summer, but can't you work that in around swim team?" asked my dad.

"No," I said. "And anyway, Coach Randall is letting me work swim team in around the 'fun,' which by the way, will also be hard work. Plus, I'll be working for Mima at the farm stand," I added. "It's not like I'll be slacking!"

My dad smiled. "You aren't capable of slacking, kid. And I love that about you. I just hate to see you toss away all your hard work in the pool. That's all."

"I don't see it that way," I said, and I folded my arms across my chest. "I see it as an investment in my future and...a kind of cross-training for swimming! I thought you guys would be all for this. I can't really believe you're giving me such a hard time. I'm so psyched to do Junior Lifeguards! Plus, it's really educational!"

My mom had picked up the papers and was reading

the program overview. "You *would* be good at it," she said thoughtfully.

"I could be just like Molly Cruise!" I said, playing my ace card. My parents had always loved Molly.

But then they exchanged a funny glance.

"What?" I asked.

"Nothing, honey," said my mom. "Look, leave the forms here. I'll talk to Amy Randall before I go to work tomorrow, and if it sounds all right, then I'll sign them and leave them here for you? Right, Dad?"

My father sighed heavily. "I guess so." He shook his head, but I pretended not to see. Their reluctance made me nervous, but I couldn't let it shake me.

"Fine," I said, ready to agree to anything that sounded like a yes.

I took a deep breath and went to study for exams, wondering vaguely what the weirdness was about Molly.

The next day was gorgeous, so my friends and I sat outside on the grass for lunch at school. Exams wouldn't start until next week, so we had a few glorious days of pretending they weren't coming. June is unpredictable on the Cape: One day it can be warm and sunny, the next day, cold and stormy. We had to take advantage of the good weather when we could.

I had spread out my hoodie and was lounging on it. Piper was next to me on her stomach, kicking her legs in the air as we chatted. Our friend Selena Diaz was there, and we were waiting for our other friend Ziggy Bloom to come back from getting her lunch out of her locker and join us. I was so happy to be with my peeps on this gorgeous day, with so much to look forward to, telling Selena all about my plans.

Selena was sitting cross-legged next to me making a daisy chain from flowers she'd pulled from a nearby bush. "Junior Lifeguards, huh?" she said. "That sounds kinda cool."

I sat bolt upright. "Do it with us!"

"Us?" moaned Piper.

I glared at her. "Shush!" I said. "Yes. Come on, Selena. It'll be so fun! On the beach, cute boys..."

"Like who?" demanded Selena, setting the daisy chain on top of her head like a crown.

Selena is gorgeous. Like, people stop and turn around to look at her on the street—she's *that* pretty. She's not very tall, but she has a great petite figure and long, long reddish-brown hair, and huge dark eyes and perfect, bright-white teeth and dimples. People tell her all the time that she looks like Cree Cicchino. She always acts like she doesn't care when people say it, but I know she enjoys the compliment; she wants to be a famous actress one day, and good looks are just another tool in her drama kit. The only bummer about Selena's looks is that boys really go for her, to the exclusion of everyone else. And she and I generally have the same taste in guys. This means that usually, when we crush on a guy, he ends up liking Selena instead.

Selena had stumped me on the boy question, since obviously I had no idea who'd be trying out. "Well, we'll have to see which boys come, but if you think about who the lifeguards are now from the older grades, then *imagine* the kinds of guys from our year who will be trying out. Not just from here, but from the other towns around. It could be epic!"

Selena grinned knowingly at me. "You have no idea, chica!" she said, wagging a finger at me. "This is false advertising!"

Hmm. Busted.

"Well, I'm sure there will be handsome guys there. It's practically a prerequisite!"

"What is?" asked Ziggy Bloom, collapsing onto the grass next to us. Her patchwork denim skirt pooled all around her and her black, springy curls blew around wildly in a gust of spring breeze. She pushed them away impatiently, her tiny, fair-skinned hands gathering them into a fat twist that she clipped up at the back of her head.

"Cool daisy crown, Leeny," she added, patting Selena on the back.

"Hey, Zigs," said Piper.

"Shalom," said Ziggy. After a family service trip to Israel last summer, this had become her go-to greeting. She unwrapped a room-temperature tofu burger and began eating it hungrily. I winced. I am a meat and potatoes person, and Ziggy's vegetarianism will always be a mystery to me. "What's a prerequisite?" she asked again.

I explained about Junior Lifeguards and boy cuteness and then we all reviewed where we stood on our summer plans. I explained about my plans for swim team, the farm stand, and Junior Lifeguards. Piper explained about Bett and the barn ultimatum.

"What about you, Selena?" asked Ziggy.

Selena took the crown off her head. "I'm dying to go to this awesome acting camp I read about that's in Michigan this summer, but it's just too expensive. On the other end of the spectrum, my dad wants me to go to *summer school!*" Selena made fake gagging noises as she told us this. She's super popular and is involved in almost everything at school extracurricularly, but she doesn't get very good grades. It makes her parents mad since they are very ambitious. "Oh, and I'm also going to volunteer at the church to help them put on their summer camp musical, as usual. But that's only two evenings a week, and it doesn't start until August." We all digested this, and then Ziggy filled us in, ticking her activities off on her fingers.

"I am going to be tracking piping plover nests for the Nature Conservancy, volunteering at the food pantry, doing a weekly beach cleanup, and meeting with my knitting group twice a week to finish up some blankets we're making for kids in homeless shelters in Boston."

"Wow!" I said. "That's really generous of you."

"And impressive," added Selena.

"My parents are pretty psyched about my plans," said Ziggy modestly, taking the last bite of her tofu burger.

"The only bummer is you'll be hanging either solo or with adults all summer," Piper pointed out.

"And it *is* a lot of work," added Selena.

"Work is fun!" said Ziggy.

"Only if you get paid, you hippie!" said Piper, grabbing Ziggy's knee and squeezing it.

"Speak for yourself, capitalist!" laughed Ziggy as she whacked Piper's hand away. Ziggy's family lived very simply and close to the land on a tiny organic farm, and other than growing a small number of crops and raising chickens and a few goats, her parents didn't really have jobs. No one could figure out how they supported themselves. Ziggy had mentioned in passing that they did a lot of bartering, but it was hard to tell. They drove a Prius, grew most of their own food, used solar energy, volunteered a lot around town, and both of them were artists. We couldn't exactly ask where they got the money for say, taxes, which was the number one expense my parents liked to complain about.

"I take that as a compliment!" said Piper, all fake-serious now.

Selena and I laughed. This was an old fight between Piper and Ziggy, and they could be pretty funny about it.

"Why don't you do Junior Lifeguards, Zigs?" I asked. "It's community service! It's basically free. It's educational, and it's all about giving back."

Ziggy raised her eyebrows. "Maybe I will. What do I have to do, and when would I have to do it?"

I explained the details and emailed the website to her from my phone. Ziggy doesn't have a phone so she can't text, but she goes to the library to check her email every day.

"I'll look into it," she said. "My schedule is pretty flexible, but I don't know how much time I could commit to it."

"There'll be good-looking boys!" I added. This was my new sales pitch.

Selena snorted. "As far as you know!"

I whacked her playfully with my lunch bag. "Listen, if

the four of us did it together, it would be awesome. That much I *do* know."

Deep down inside, I prayed that I would find those forms signed and waiting for me on the kitchen table when I got home later. Who knew how the conversation had gone with my mom and Coach Randall earlier? It would just be so embarrassing if I convinced all my friends to do it and then I wasn't allowed to do it myself!

"Well, so far, it's just the one of us. But we might come cheer you on at tryouts, Jenna. Right, girls?" said Piper.

The bell rang to signal the start of the next period. We all stood up and began to pack up our stuff and gather our trash. Selena and Ziggy moved off toward the garbage area, with its compost and recycling bins.

"Baby steps, Pipester! Baby steps!" I teased.

Suddenly, Piper pulled me aside and whispered, "Jenna, even if I did want to do it, you have to face the fact that I would probably fail the test. Don't you see that? Why would I bother humiliating myself? Think about it."

She took off for her next class, and I stood there, open-mouthed, digesting this information. Piper was a great athlete. But would she pass? I wasn't sure. Did I still think she should go for it? Selfishly, yes. But for her own sake? A good friend would say no. So, what did that make me?

4

Boys

I raced into the kitchen after school and sure enough, there were the forms, all filled out, with a check sitting next to them.

"Yahoo!" I cried. I couldn't believe it! I felt so lucky right then to have all these adults in my life who were helping me have a great summer. I closed my eyes briefly in gratitude. "Thank you, Coach Randall," I whispered out loud. I wondered what she had said to my mom to convince her.

I picked up the landline and dialed Piper's cell. It

rang three times, and just when I was about to hang up, she answered.

"It's me!" I gasped. "I'm going to turn in my forms and check for the tryouts. Did you get Bett to sign yours?"

There was a brief silence at the other end of the phone. Then Piper said flatly, "Yes. But Bett and I just had a fight about it. I still don't want to do it. But she said I had to at least go through the tryouts. If I don't make it, then that's that."

I paused. Then I said, "I think that's fair. It's worth a shot, Pipe. Come on. Just come meet me at Lookout Beach now. I'll wait for you there!" I said.

Was I being too forceful? I couldn't tell. I always had to push Piper: she never wanted to do new things or go to new places, but once she tried them, she always liked them. I'm sure that was part of what Bett was hoping to cure her of by "firing" her for the summer. And selfishly, it *would* be great if everything worked out for us to both do Junior Lifeguards together. Because of swim team, I never get to do enough stuff with my school friends, and

Junior Lifeguards would be more fun with a buddy. If Ziggy and Selena did it too, well, that would just be icing on the cake.

There was silence at the other end of the phone.

Finally, Piper sighed loudly. "Why do I let you drag me into these things?"

"Because you love me, and you know I'm right!" I crowed. I did a little dance of happiness.

"I'll see you there in half an hour," said Piper morosely, and she hung up.

"*Yes!*" I pumped my fist, squashing my fears about her passing the swim test. I just wasn't going to think about it. I put the phone back in the cradle, and just then, a notepad on the counter caught my eye. It was my mom's handwriting.

MC. Saint Sebastian's Rehab Center. 114 Old Oak Highway, Barnstable.

I wondered what that was. Who needed rehab, and what was MC? I flipped the pages but there was nothing else. Weird. I wondered if it was something from her conversation with Coach Randall.

Speaking of Coach Randall, it sure felt funny to be home at this time of day when I'd usually be at swim practice. My brothers were still out, my parents were at work, and I had the house all to myself. It was a little lonely but also kind of liberating. I felt like leaping around on the furniture in my underwear! (Kidding!)

As I gathered my things to head out the door, a small *new* worry popped into my mind: What if Piper failed the test on purpose?

Lookout Beach was basically empty, except for the occasional car pulling up to check out the waves and a couple of bikes in the bike rack. One was Ziggy's, and I could see her off in the dunes, a huge black garbage bag in one hand and a pair of superlong tongs in the other. She was doing a beach cleanup. The beaches in Westham always look clean to me, but Ziggy always says we'd be surprised at what she picks up every week on trash duty, especially once the busy tourist season starts after the Fourth of July.

I stashed my bike in the rack and headed onto the broad porch that wrapped around the Lookout Beach pavilion. The pavilion has a shop with a snack bar (where Selena's older brother, Hugo, works in the summer), lockers and showers, and the main beach office. The porch has picnic tables and benches spread out and was, at the moment, totally empty. On a bustling August Saturday, this place would be packed—every table and chair taken and a line out the door of the snack bar. I like it both ways—crowded and empty—though when it's empty, I usually wish it were crowded, and vice versa!

The office door stuck a little from the sea air, and when I shoved it, the bell above the door jangled wildly and I crashed into the room, mortified. The three people working inside all looked up in surprise as I entered.

"Hi!" I waved, turning beet red.

Instantly, I realized that one of the people was Luke Slater, the cute blond guy I'd seen hanging the posters that day at the Y. I could feel myself turning redder as he grinned at me.

"Can we help you?" asked an older woman nicely.

"Uh... I'm here about, um, Junior Lifeguards?" I stammered. I knew immediately whom I'd come to see, but I didn't want him to think I was a stalker by recognizing him.

"That's Luke," she sighed, turning back to her desk and jerking her thumb toward the blond guy. I looked at her desk and saw she worked for the local conservation group. There were photos all over her bulletin board of birds in various states of distress and fliers and signs for environmental events. I was sure that was who Ziggy was outside working for, and somehow, I knew Luke got lots more customers than she did. On *his* bulletin board, there were tons of photos of kids in red bathing suits doing athletic-looking stuff on a sunny beach. I was sure my old sitter Molly was in some of the photos.

I glanced at Luke and saw that he was waving at me.

"Yoo-hoo!" he joked. "Over here!"

I laughed and crossed the room to his desk. "Hi, I'm Jenna Bowers and I am interested in signing up for Junior Lifeguards for this summer." I'd rehearsed what I'd say as I rode here, but I realized my mistake as soon as it was out of my mouth.

"Well, uh, actually, you don't sign up," said Luke, kindly. "You kinda have to try out? But I'm sure you'll make it, a swim team girl like you, so don't worry!" he added.

Ugh. I'd known that, obvs, and now I sounded totally presumptuous. But more importantly, *he* recognized *me*! "Wait, how did you know..." I stammered, as I found myself blushing again for both reasons.

"Saw you at the Y that day," he said, ducking his head

so I couldn't see his eyes as he reached into a file cabinet for some paperwork.

"Oh! Right! Was that you?" I fibbed.

"Yup!" he said, coming back up. He smacked some papers onto his desk and grinned again. "That was me! Luke Slater. Nice to meet you." He put out his hand and I shook it.

Now I knew *he* knew that I knew it was him, but what could I say? Oh boy. I'd played it all wrong. I hoped he didn't think I was rude. I had to squint at him and mutter something noncommittal, like, "Oh... Jenna Bowers. Nice to meet you too."

Luke continued. "Here are the forms you'll need to fill out."

"Oh, I already did that. Here," I said, pulling my little string backpack off my shoulders and withdrawing my filled in paperwork and check.

"Great!" said Luke. I could tell he was kind of impressed, which was good. Maybe that would offset the fact that I had just acted like I could just sign up without a tryout and that I'd "forgotten" that I'd seen him before. *Great start, Bowers,* I told myself.

I laid the paperwork out on the table, thrilled again at seeing my mom's loopy signature of approval on the page. I looked up at Luke, who was studying it. It took him a moment longer than I would have thought, but I guess he was being thorough. Or maybe he was just trying to torture me by making me think it might not be complete? I'd deserve it, if so. Hmm.

But then, "Good. This is all set. I'll just run it by our program director when he gets in, but I think you're good to go. You'll be able to make the tryout this Saturday at the Y?" He smacked his forehead. "Oh! Wait! Do you have a meet you have to go to up the Cape?"

Oh dear. Here it comes. The explaining!

"I, uh, actually, I'm sort of taking the summer off from swim team? I mean, I'm doing a modified schedule. So... I'll be...very free?" I had almost said *available,* and now I couldn't tell which was worse. Did it sound like I was trying to say I was available for dating or something? But he was way older than I am. He was like sixteen or maybe even seventeen.

"Oh. Okay. Great, then," he said. But I knew that inside, his wheels were turning, like *I'll need to check up on this one and see if she was kicked off swim team for some reason.*

I exhaled slowly. I guess this was the beginning of my "new normal," post–swim team life. What else could I expect?

"Well, this looks like it's all set then!" Luke said brightly.

"Thanks! So. Great! Um..."

"Thanks for coming in," said Luke, standing up. He folded his arms and smiled, and right then, the door banged open and the bell went crazy again.

"Piper!" I cried. There was no one on earth I would rather have seen right then!

"Hey," she said shyly, trying to close the door quietly behind her. The conservation lady and the lady at the parking desk looked over and looked away, instantly knowing whom Piper was there to see.

"Piper Janssens, this is Luke Slater," I began, feeling more confident now.

"Hi," said Piper with a small smile. She looked away and then looked back at Luke, like he was the sun and she was being blinded by him.

"Hi," he said. "Welcome!"

"Piper wants to try out for Junior Lifeguards too!" I said.

"Great! The more, the merrier," said Luke. "Did you already do your paperwork too?"

Piper nodded and handed it over. I could see Bett's neat signature on the paperwork and the check.

"Good job, Pipe," I whispered. She glared at me out of the corner of her eye as Luke studied everything. Again, it took a little while, during which Piper glanced at me nervously and I gestured very minorly with my hand that she should be patient, everything was fine.

Finally, Luke looked up brightly. "This is all set too! Wow. You're the most organized kids who've come in yet!"

I beamed, like he'd told me I was a genius or looked like a model or something. Piper looked at me with wide eyes, and then she said, "So, all we have to do now is the...swim test?"

"Yup! Two tests. Pool and then ocean. Piece of cake for two athletic girls like you!" he said.

"Oh, I'm not..." Piper started to protest. But luckily, I didn't have to stomp on her foot to shut her up, because right then the bell jingled ever so gently and Ziggy Bloom appeared, closing the door quietly behind her.

"Hey! Look who's here!" Ziggy cried, pleasantly surprised by our presence. "Hang on a sec!"

She crossed to the conservation lady, and they had a quick conference on what Ziggy had seen and found in the dunes. The lady clearly adored Ziggy, but then again, most people did. Ziggy finished her report as we stood there waiting, and then she crossed back to us and said, "Hey, man!" to Luke.

"What *up*, Zigs?" he joked, picking her up off her feet and swinging her a little bit in a hug. "Are these girls friends of yours?"

Piper's eyes nearly popped out of her head at the display of affection between Ziggy and Luke.

Ziggy smiled at Piper and me like a proud mother. "Yep. I raised them up from pupu," she joked.

"Well done!" Luke joked back. It was weird to see that they were such good friends and so comfortable together, considering she had never even mentioned him to us.

"Hey, so should *I* try out?" asked Ziggy.

At first Luke laughed, but then he realized Ziggy wasn't joking, and he got all serious, fast. "Oh, sure! Yeah. Totally! You should come out. Especially, if all your friends are doing it. The...uh...swim test is a *little* tough. I mean... not terrible, or anything. At all! But just..."

Ziggy laughed. "I know, I know, I'm not as jocky as

these two. But I can swim. And I have great instincts in the water, my dad always says. I think I might go for it."

"Cool! Here's the paperwork." Luke handed it all over.

"Saves you a trip to the library," I said.

"Yeah!" she smiled.

"So, if you have any questions, or if there's anything I can do for you, just give me a call. My number's on the sheet," said Luke.

"Cool," I echoed.

Piper grinned and blushed again. "See you around..."

"See you in three days!" corrected Luke with a smile, and he pointed his finger at us.

"Right," nodded Piper, still grinning broadly.

"Bye, dude," said Ziggy with a wave.

Outside, by unspoken mutual agreement, we walked very quickly to the table and chairs farthest from the office and then collapsed into giggles.

"OMG, he is so cute!" cried Piper. "How am I going to swim in front of someone like that?"

"I can't believe you know that guy, and you've never even mentioned him to us!" I said to Ziggy.

Ziggy shrugged. "I guess I don't think of him that way. He's not really my type."

"What, you don't like good-looking guys who are nice and friendly too?" joked Piper, but she was kind of indignant.

"Yeah, I don't know... I don't really go for the all-American type, you know? The whole blond-haired, blue-eyed varsity athlete look? I mean, don't get me wrong, I can see he's adorable! But it's not what floats my boat."

Piper was shaking her head in amazement, but I had to agree with Ziggy.

"I guess I prefer dark-haired, dark-eyed guys too," I said. "And guys who are taller..."

Piper's eyes suddenly got all mischievous. "What?" I said.

She wiggled her eyebrows. "Like him?" she whispered, looking meaningfully over my shoulder.

I whipped around just in time for a tall, dark, and handsome teenage guy to catch me checking him out. He was dressed kind of preppy—khaki shorts and a ratty Vineyard Vines T-shirt, a rope belt around his shorts, and no socks with his Sperry Top-Siders. He smiled a little as we locked eyes, then he pushed open the door to the beach office.

"Seriously? You couldn't have said he was looking right at us? Thanks, Piper. Now that guy totally knows I was checking him out," I said, dropping my head into my hands in mortification. I could feel my face burning. "He basically laughed in my face!"

"Oh, stop your drama. I'm sorry for doing that, but wasn't he a contender?" pressed Piper.

I looked up. "Of course!"

"So?" laughed Piper.

Ziggy was laughing too. "I like 'em dark and handsome, but that guy was just *too* tall."

"Maybe you're *too* short!" I teased. I am five feet seven

inches already, and my doctor says I've still got a few inches to go. This height is great for swimming but not for dating boys my age who haven't grown yet, so I have to keep my sights set high—height-wise, that is.

"Guys!" a voice called from the parking lot.

"Can I turn around this time?" I joked.

"Leeny!" called Ziggy.

I turned. Selena was crossing from the top of the parking lot to the porch to come see us. She had some papers in her hand.

"What's up, sister?" I said.

Selena plunked down at our table and groaned dramatically. She laid one of the sheets out on the table, and we could all see it was a Junior Lifeguards application, all filled in.

"Yay! Selena's doing it!" I dove at her for a sideways hug, which she accepted, but not with enthusiasm.

"My brother brought the flyer home from work the other day, and that idiot showed it to my parents before he even checked with me, and now they're all over this. My mom made me walk over to submit my application and fee!" Selena waved a white business envelope at us unhappily.

"But wait, I'm confused. I thought you might *want* to do this with us!" I said.

Selena sighed wearily, her face a mask of displeasure. "I *guess* so. It's just that it seems a little like school, and it also means for sure that I don't get to go to acting camp." She folded her arms on the table and rested her cheek on them in a pretty pout. "And now my dad says I have to go to the library all summer and get tutored."

Ziggy patted her on the back. "I love the library! Lifeguards will be great too. Don't worry, we'll have fun," she said.

"Are *you* doing it?" asked Selena, lifting her head in surprise.

Ziggy smiled. "Maybe! I just have to show this to my mom when she comes, which is right now! Mommy!

Mommy! Over here!" she yelled across the porch as her mother pulled up in her Prius.

"Zigs, seriously, *Mommy*?" said Pipe in a strangled whisper. "Shhh!"

I glanced around. "No one heard," I told Piper, rolling my eyes.

"She loves it when I call her that," said Ziggy, standing to go to her car. "It's how I can get her to say yes to things." She tapped her head. "Always thinking."

Piper glanced around, obviously checking for the boys, "Not thinking *that* hard," she muttered as Ziggy walked away.

"So, Selena," Piper began. "It looks like this Junior Lifeguard thing is Cute Guy City!"

"Hmmm," said Selena dubiously.

I nodded. "It's true. Already, we've seen two really handsome guys..."

"Yeah, and Ziggy's already friends with one of them!" crowed Piper.

I glanced at Ziggy in the parking lot and did a double take. She was fighting with her mom, gesturing wildly with her arms and practically stomping her foot.

"What's up with Ziggy?" I asked the others.

Piper half stood, as if to go over to her, but I put my hand on her arm. It didn't look like now was the time to intrude.

"She's freaking out," said Piper.

"Yes, she is pitching a total fit," agreed Selena.

We were all staring at Ziggy, and then suddenly, a deep voice behind me said, "Hello, Junior Lifeguards!"

The Residents of Brookfield Lane

I turned around and had to look up, up, up! It was the tall guy who'd busted me checking him out before. I blushed immediately.

"Hi!" said Selena in her naturally flirty way, dimples and all, and I found myself a little annoyed by her friendliness.

"Oh, we're not Junior Lifeguards—" said Piper.

"Yet!" I corrected, and the guy laughed. "Well, neither am I, but it would be fun if we all made it. I'm Hayden Jones," he said, grinning at us all.

I smiled back. "Hi. I'm Jenna Bowers, and these are my friends Piper and Selena."

"Hi all," he said, rocking on his heels. "Why's your friend freaking out in the parking lot?" he asked, tipping his chin toward Ziggy.

"We don't know..." said Piper.

"Yet!" I added, and this time we all laughed.

"Is that all you can say?" he teased.

He *was* tall, probably around six feet, and dark, with tan skin and dark wavy hair and chocolaty brown eyes under thick dark eyebrows. He had very white teeth and a little dimple high on his cheek that only came out when he smiled—*very* handsome. Because of his messy preppy outfit, he looked like a lot of the summer kids around here, so I figured him for one immediately.

"Where are you from?" I asked, matching his boldness with my own. There was something about him that made me feel instantly comfortable, and he had an energy and sense of humor that were contagious.

He narrowed his eyes at me. "What makes you think I'm not from here?"

"Um, that I don't already know you?" I said.

"Oh, good one. Good detective work," said Hayden, laughing and shaking a finger at me. "Well, I'm originally from Greenwich, Connecticut. Then my parents got divorced, and I moved to..." He stopped and looked at me with a grin. "Wait, do you want the long version or the short version?"

"How about short for now?" I said, matching his grin with my own.

"Fine, but then I get to corner you one day and tell you the whole story, okay? Maybe over an ice-cream cone?"

"Deal," I said. I couldn't believe how flirty we were being. This was soooo not like me!

"I am from Palm Beach, Florida. Currently."

"Okay. Cool. That must be fun. So why are you here now? Shouldn't you be at home in school?"

Hayden paused for a second, and then shook his head.

"We get out early in the South. Too hot for school." He glanced away, a little uneasily, I thought. Hmm.

I looked at Piper and Selena, but they seemed to be engrossed in watching Ziggy, who had started to cry.

"Maybe now would be a good time for us to go over there?" suggested Piper.

"I'll hand in my app then meet you over there," agreed Selena, rising from the bench. Reluctantly, I stood up to join Piper.

"So, you'll be at the test this weekend, then?" asked Hayden Jones, boy cutie.

"Yup," I nodded. *Thank goodness I'm a great swimmer,* I thought. *With guys like him and even Luke around, it's going to be pretty distracting.* I didn't want to leave him, but I did think I should go see what was happening with Ziggy.

"Anyway..." I began, right as Hayden was saying, "So..."

We both laughed, and Hayden put out his hand. "It was good to meet you, Jenna Bowers," he said, fake formally.

"Good to meet you too, Hayden Jones." I reached out to

shake his hand and felt a jolt of electricity when our hands clasped. His hand was much larger than mine, and warm and kind of rough. I blushed and let go pretty quickly. How embarrassing.

"See you this weekend..." said Hayden, as I began to walk away to catch up with the others.

"Bye!" I called back over my shoulder, my face aflame. What was wrong with me? It was just a handshake!

Part of me wanted desperately to stay and keep talking to Hayden, but I can only carry on that kind of flirtiness for a short while before I get embarrassed or my brain gets tired of trying to be fun and jazzy and say the right thing every time.

I reached the car, and Ziggy had stopped crying, but her face was tear-stained and she was pleading with her mother.

Ziggy's mom waved out the car window. "Hi, Jenna," she said softly.

"Hi Mrs., um...Lisa!" I said awkwardly. Ziggy's mom

was insistent people not call her Mrs. Bloom, which she said was a title that oppressed women by implying their husband's ownership of them or something. Ziggy said it was because Lisa had never liked her mother-in-law so didn't want to share a name with her. I ended up calling her Mrs. Lisa all the time.

Ziggy was in the middle of a fervent speech. "Luke said you can make money lifeguarding at kids' pool parties and also babysitting. He said it looks really good to the parents if you know lifesaving, and all the kids in the program can make a lot of money during the off-hours, if they do that stuff," said Ziggy.

I followed Ziggy's lead and added, "Oh, I saw a flyer in the office that said Brewster is looking for pool guards at their rec center, and they pay seventeen dollars an hour! We could do that in a year or two when we're certified!"

"What's all this talk about money?" asked Ziggy's mom, disdainfully. Ziggy's parents sometimes seemed to think money was their enemy. "Capitalism is a very flawed system. The one percent of super-wealthy people rule the poor and..."

"Mom!" Ziggy rolled her eyes.

"Well, Junior Lifeguards is just the first step in a multi-year program that results in being a full ocean guard," I said, looking at Ziggy. She nodded. "It pays really well in the end." I continued. "My old babysitter Molly Cruise did it and she got a great job lifeguarding right here!"

"So, this is basically *Baywatch* for beginners?" Ziggy's mom chuckled at her own joke, but none of us knew what she was talking about.

"What's *Baywatch*?" asked Ziggy, annoyed.

"Oh, it was just this silly show about lifeguards that was on television when I was a kid. Lots of half-naked bimbos and dopey guys with muscles, pulling people out of the ocean. Thank God we don't have a TV anymore." Mrs. Lisa rolled her eyes.

"The Slaters aren't bimbos or dopes," said Ziggy indignantly.

"Oh, please, Ziggy. Don't you remember how that Bud Slater spoke so aggressively at the town meeting about the plover nesting areas?" said Ziggy's mom.

I thought maybe I should try a different tactic. "Uh, it's a great experience, Mrs. Lisa. It would look really good on Ziggy's college applications and stuff later."

"Oh, honey, that's so nice, but we don't... Ziggy's father and I don't want her to live her life chained to some list of expectations from colleges... We just aren't into that."

"Oh. Okay," I said. I couldn't imagine parents *not* being "into that." It was kind of weird.

"Ziggy thinks it would be really fun," offered Piper, smiling encouragingly at Ziggy.

"Really, love? I can't believe you think it would be fun. It's so not you," said Mrs. Lisa to Ziggy, and she handed her back the sheet.

"How do you know what's me or not? You always tell me to follow my bliss!" stormed Ziggy.

This was getting ugly, and all of our arguments were

not getting Ziggy anywhere. I looked at Selena and Piper, and we all agreed with our eyes; it was time for us to go.

"This is not *bliss*," said her mom, sitting up straight in her seat. "This is a bunch of jocks running around in bathing suits in the hot sun all day, competing to win the approval of the dumbest jock of all, that Bud Slater."

"Mom! That is so rude! Jenna and Piper and Selena are all doing it!" yelled Ziggy.

"Zigs, I...uh...think we're going to hit the road, okay? Sorry," I said nervously. "Bye, Mrs....Lisa!"

Selena and Piper said their goodbyes, and we grabbed our two bikes and by silent agreement began walking Selena home.

We waited until we were a few hundred feet down the hill of the beach parking lot and onto Ocean Road to say anything, but then we couldn't keep any of it in.

"Mrs. Bloom is a phony!" Piper said angrily. "She always pretends to be so cool and chill, but the second Ziggy wants to do something different from her parents' agenda, Mrs. Bloom gets all uptight about it. I hate it when adults think they know better than us. Everything they want us to do or not do is like the *opposite* of what we want!" We merged from the street onto the sidewalk, and Piper kicked a pebble angrily.

"Yeah, like making us try out for Junior Lifeguards instead of going away to a beautiful acting camp," moped Selena.

"Or quitting the barn to go drown in front of lots of cute guys," added Piper.

I wanted to join in on this topic, but I'd lately had a bunch of adults actually *help* me do some things I really wanted to do. I didn't have a leg to stand on. I looked up at the fresh green tree leaves arcing over our heads as I tried to gather my thoughts.

"I guess...they don't want to see us make mistakes.

They want to see us be happy but also not waste our time or energy on the wrong things."

"What *they* think are the wrong things!" said Piper, her eyes flashing. She yanked a handful of beach plum leaves off a bush as we passed and began ripping the soft, pale green foliage into confetti that she trailed out of her loosely opened fingers as we walked.

I shrugged. "Sometimes they're right, though."

"I hate it when that happens," said Selena in a voice so tragic that Piper and I had to laugh.

"So, how about those two guys?" I asked, trying to lighten the mood.

Piper's eyes lit up. "Luke is really cute. He's too old for us, but still..."

Selena nodded. "Yes. Both attractive," she agreed. I listened carefully for any sign of interest, hoping she wouldn't show any in Hayden in particular. If we both ended up liking the same boy, there was no contest about who would win. And I was definitely a little interested in him.

"Ooh, look! Honeysuckle!" cried Selena. It rambled over a low fence and onto the path, its creamy blossoms bursting with scent. We stopped to pull some of the flowers off so we could nip off the ends of them and get at the sweet nectar inside.

Casually, between sips of honeysuckle juice, I said, "So what *did* you guys think of that guy, Hayden?" I flicked away the spent flower and picked a new one.

"Cute!" said Piper, but that wasn't saying much. She thinks pretty much every boy with a pulse is "cute."

"Yes, very handsome," agreed Selena. Uh-oh. That was a pretty strong statement. "A little sketchy, maybe?" She busily looked along the vine for an open flower to pluck, so I couldn't see her face.

"Oh. Yeah, uh-huh, hmmm," I said in a noncommittal tone. How on earth had Selena sensed that too? She'd only spoken to him for thirty seconds! But it was annoying Selena had picked up on it; I realized now that I was trying to ignore that vibe from him, to bury my instincts because he was so handsome. Aargh! I was frustrated. Should I ask Selena *why* she thought that or just leave it alone? I didn't really want to know; I just wanted to like him.

"That's all," said Selena, examining the vine. We set out walking again, this time in companionable silence for a minute.

For swim team, Coach Randall used to make us practice mindfulness: living in the moment, observing our surroundings. I tried it now, just to keep myself from obsessing over the boy. It always helps with stuff like this.

I took in the shushing sound of the waves at the beach behind me, the repetitive squeak of Piper's tight brake pad on her front bike wheel, the bright blue of the sky, and the still-warm sun on our shoulders. We turned left off Ocean Road to Brookfield Lane, the fanciest street in town, where the big estates were. Here, the aroma of freshly mowed lawns mingled with puffs of diesel fumes from the tractors, hedge trimmers, and pickup trucks of the landscapers parked all up and down the street, tending to the fancy properties. There were no sidewalks on this country lane, so we walked on the edge of the road where the asphalt and grass met in a wavering line.

I studied the blooming roses that rambled over the white picket fence in front of the huge estate to my left. Each rose was a bright, cheerful red bloom, burst wide open on its fresh green stem, not a dead leaf or brown petal in sight. Beyond the fence, a rolling green lawn rose like a carpet to a huge white-shingled house with crisp black shutters on its dozens of windows.

"Pretty," I said.

Piper and Selena glanced over to see what I was looking at.

"Yeah. It's like a museum or something," said Piper.

Selena started to say something, but then closed her mouth and almost imperceptibly shook her head.

"What?" I asked, not missing a trick. Selena always had lots of gossip on the rich people who lived on Brookfield Lane. As a resident of the street and as the daughter of recent immigrants who'd prospered and found work and beautiful lodging at one of the houses, Selena had both an insider's *and* an outsider's perspective. Plus, her mom and dad knew a lot of the other people from Ecuador who worked up and down the street. News traveled fast in this tight community of people looking after the super-rich.

"Come on!" I insisted. "Now you have to tell us!"

Selena rolled her eyes and laughed. "You always push me into telling you stuff, and then I regret it later. It's not appropriate for me to repeat stuff. My parents are always scolding us about this."

"It's been ages since you've had something juicy about the summer people! Just tell us! It's not like we know any of them!" I implored her.

"Well, some of them we know, maybe, like from the barn or from the farm stand," said Piper.

"Shush, Piper! You're not helping my case!" I chided, jokingly.

Selena smiled. "It's been ages because it's been winter

and none of them were here. Okay. This is a weird one, and I'm sure it's not true. You can't repeat it, no matter what, because if anyone hears it and it comes back to me..." For all her protesting, Selena's flashing eyes and the dramatic toss of her long, caramel-streaked hair indicated she was enjoying her role in sharing the drama. She always did.

"Yeah, yeah, yeah, who are we going to tell?" I said dismissively. "Let's go."

We had stopped on the edge of the road, and I gazed at the enormous house again. To the side, was a perfectly manicured putting green and beyond it a pool and a huge guest house (bigger than my real house). Droopy blue blooms were beginning to appear on the bushy hydrangeas that surrounded the foundation of the house. Every window sparkled in the late afternoon sun. Someday, I would love to live in a house like that. I just had to figure out how.

Selena took a deep breath and waited until Piper and I were both looking at her.

"Okay, I heard..."

Just then a massive green Range Rover came careening around the corner from Ocean onto Brookfield, techno music blaring out of its open windows. As it roared past us, I spied a gorgeous, blond twentysomething guy behind the wheel in golden Ray-Bans and a pale pink polo shirt over huge tan biceps; there were also two young girls with wildly curly long dark hair, one seated in the front and one in the back.

As the car roared past us, the horn tooted three times in greeting.

"What the..." said Piper in annoyance.

"Wow!" I said, jumping back onto the grass along the roadside.

Selena stayed stock still, staring after the car. It went about a hundred yards further and turned into Selena's driveway.

"Who was that?" demanded Piper.

Selena's mouth had dropped open. She turned to us as if just waking from a dream.

And then: "The Frankel girls are here," she said solemnly.

My mouth dropped open in shock. "Now? That was them? Just there?" I craned my head to see if I could see more, but they were gone, a cloud of gravel dust hanging in the air at the end of the driveway was the only sign they'd been there.

Selena began trudging toward where they had just disappeared, her shoulders drooping, and her head hanging sadly.

"Leeny?" said Piper, scrambling to catch up.

"My summer is officially over," said Selena morosely.

"Um..." I didn't know what to say. I mean, I knew that Selena lived in the massive gatehouse of the massively more massive Frankel estate (Sir David Frankel was a major Russian billionaire by way of London; Lady Jemima Frankel was a Somali model turned CNN newscaster, always broadcasting from some war-torn place, looking gorgeous in a khaki flak jacket and black headscarf). I'd always understood that the whole estate—which we usually had the run of—belonged to someone else who rarely came. We were always aware they existed. We thought about them briefly the first few moments we jumped on their trampoline or swam in their pool. It was just that after a few years of having it all to ourselves, the Frankels had begun to seem like a fictitious family.

And now they were actually here.

We'd reached the end of the driveway, which was so long you couldn't even see the house from the end of it.

"Guys, I'm going to head in on my own, okay?" said Selena sadly.

"Are you okay?" asked Piper, her face wrinkled with concern.

Selena nodded. "It just takes some adjusting. And my mom will need my help. You know..."

"See you tomorrow?" I asked.

Selena nodded. "I'll be at school. And the tryouts on

Saturday, of course," she added, the picture of sadness as she turned to go.

"Leeny?" I couldn't help myself. I just had to know. "What were you going to tell us before, about that mansion?" I asked her as she walked away from us.

Selena stopped, partway up the driveway, her back to us. It was clear she was deciding whether or not to tell us what she knew. After a pause, without turning around, she said, "I heard it belongs to Ziggy's grandparents." And she began walking again, up the long, bluestone driveway, bordered on each side by a perfectly squared off privet hedge, rising ten feet high on either side of her.

6

Background Check

That night, after my homework was finished and I'd done extra practice on my math and made a Quizlet for my Latin vocabulary, I finally had some time to myself. So, I did what any normal teenager with free time does: I got busy googling.

The Frankels were my first target, and what I found was a gold mine. There was tons of professional and social information about the Frankel parents—the mom—gorgeous supermodel-turned-newscaster, Imari—at parties with the Dalai Lama, the head of Israel, miscellaneous rich Russian people in London, and so on. The dad—older, toadish-looking, expensively dressed, Benjamin—was pictured in business meetings with people, touring factories, cheering for his championship tier "football club" in England (and by "his," it meant he owned it). It was kind of interesting, but not as interesting as the things I found about the Frankel girls, Samantha and Alessandra.

Samantha and Alessandra were born eleven months apart, making them "Irish twins," the same age for a month each year. They seemed to be inseparable and were as beautiful and stylish as their mother. There were some vague and hazy older siblings from the dad's first two marriages who drifted in and out of the photos I found, but none were as attractive and none were as photographed as the two youngest girls; the ones I'd seen in the car today on Brookfield Lane. Among the things I saw were: the sisters at a polo match with the Queen of England, Princess Catherine, and miscellaneous British royalty, all in fancy hats; the sisters (looking much younger) at a fundraiser carnival, each carrying a massive Hello Kitty balloon; the sisters and their parents stepping off their private jet in Tokyo with Taylor Swift; and the sisters holding matching baby lion cubs at a game preserve in their mom's native Somalia. Another thing I saw were multiple photos of the girls with a tan, blond hunk named Nigel Tompkins, who I could almost say for sure was the guy in the pink polo shirt who'd been driving the car today. He appeared to be their babysitter—or "manny" as the London magazines called him—and he was in just as many pictures with the sisters as their parents were—maybe even more.

My eyes were bulging out of my head by the time I had finished googling. What a life these people had: endless travel and wealth, mingling with the rich and famous, and looking incredible all the while. I almost felt sick from it, like I'd eaten too much candy.

I sat back in my desk chair and swiveled from side to side, looking out the window behind my loft bed to the lights of the neighbors' house not fifty feet outside my window. What would it be like to live with all that excitement, all those houses and destinations and parties? I couldn't imagine, though I was sure I would enjoy it. What stumped me was why would they add Westham to all that? I mean, sure, the landscape, the light, the beaches—they're all beautiful. And historically, Westham was a very mellow fishing community with friendly people where you could get away from it all. Now it is an overpopulated mess, with mega-mansions built in every former field, minor celebrities crowding the nightlife, and gridlock in town on the weekends. I guess if you are a see-and-be-seen type of social person, Westham is a natural destination. But to bother to own a house here? And so far from London? How did the Frankels even start coming here and why?

I rubbed my eyes and considered the girls I'd seen in the Range Rover. Were they excited to be back in Westham? Did they have favorite things to do here that they were looking forward to, like mini-golf and drive-in movies and lobster bakes? Was Nigel happy to be here with them? How would they spend their time here, and how long would they stay?

I looked back at my computer and my fingers hovered over the keys. What I really wanted to know about now was the Bloom family history. But the problem is this: I am a terrible liar. If I found out something about Ziggy that she hadn't told me herself, I would have a hard time acting naturally if she ever mentioned it. Like, what if I saw a picture of her and her parents with the head of Israel, and then Ziggy mentioned something like, "Hey, did you know I met the head of Israel?" and I'd be all awkward, like, "No way! *Really?*" but I would blush, and she would totally know I already knew.

I closed my computer. For now, I wouldn't do any googling of the Blooms. Maybe if I listened carefully, I'd learn from the people around me. Maybe even Ziggy would tell us things herself. Or maybe I could get some backstory from some very savvy sources, if I played my cards right, that is.

Dinner at my aunt Ginny's is usually a free-for-all. On my mom's side alone, I have twelve cousins of all ages who live in or near Westham, plus three aunts, two uncles, and my grandma. When Ginny hosts a family dinner, the food is always amazing, since she's the chef who does the prepared food for the family farm stand. The setting is always casual open-house buffet, with people coming and going all evening. My aunt Suzie (she's married to my mom's brother, Jackson) brings dessert, which is guaranteed to be awesome too. She's the one who bakes for our family farm stand, and her blueberry cobblers are legendary every August when it's blueberry season on the Cape. It was strawberry season, so she was deep into strawberry rhubarb pies these days.

I love going to my aunt's and seeing everyone, but I hate getting stuck watching the little kids when all I want to do is hear the adults' gossip. This night was worse than usual; even though twenty-four hours had passed, I was still burning with questions about the Slaters, the Blooms, and the Frankels. I knew that with all their connections in the area, someone in my family would have answers. But who? And how could I get their attention long enough to find out?

"Mom," I interrupted. She was sitting with my aunt Ginny and their other, much younger sister, Callie.

"Jen, honey, can you please watch Téa and the twins while Callie finishes eating?" said my mom. Callie's daughter Téa was six, and my twin brothers, Finn and Gavin, were seven. The three of them were inseparable and pretty rowdy together.

I sighed. I'd just been watching them for twenty minutes on the swing set out back, and it already felt like an hour.

"It's okay, Jenna, leave them be for a minute and come sit," said my aunt Callie, scooting over and patting the spot on the ottoman next to her. "Come tell us about Junior Lifeguards. I always wanted to do it when I was your age."

I wanted to hug Callie right then; she was a mind reader. It was just the introduction I needed.

"Well, it hasn't really started yet. I just put in my application yesterday..."

"Down at Lookout Beach?" asked Ginny, balancing her dinner plate on her knee. Ginny was the second oldest of all my mom's siblings; her kids were in college, so she'd kind of seen it all in Westham.

I nodded. "Yup, with Luke Slater? And I guess his dad runs it. Bud Slater or something?"

"Oh, boy! The Slaters!" Ginny rolled her eyes and hooted. Then she shook her head and continued eating.

"What?" I asked, all innocent, but hoping for some dirt.

"Nothing," said my mom, shaking her head. "They're perfectly nice."

"Depends on who you ask!" giggled Ginny.

"Why?" I said. I had to be careful not to push or my

mother would get annoyed by my nosiness and send me outside to watch the kids. Ginny, on the other hand, loved a good gossip, and Callie always had an interesting perspective on things since she was basically a half generation in between my mom and me.

"You know, small-town stuff. Old news." My mom shrugged dismissively. My mom does not like to gossip. Not at all. It was a major shortcoming in a mother, as far as I was concerned. How was I supposed to learn anything?

Ginny rolled her eyes. "Okay, Carol Slater, Luke's mom—originally Carol Tansey—was from here. Nice family. Salt of the earth. Her mom was our school nurse, right? In grade school?"

My mom nodded, not willing to contribute even one word to Ginny's storytelling.

Ginny continued. "Her dad was a lineman for the power company. Great guy. Volunteer firefighter, really charitable. A rock. Anyway, that Bud Slater rolled into town one summer from Beacon Hill—spoiled, rich, good-looking—"

"Well, he wasn't rich anymore," said my mom.

I was shocked. She was contributing! I hunched my head down into my shoulders and sealed my lips—if they forgot I was there, they would say more.

"Right," agreed Ginny. "He was a summer kid, and his dad was a drunk and lost all the money they inherited from the grandparents, so they had to move out here full time to some shack, and Bud enrolled in Westham High; it was a real comedown for him and his family. Then his parents split up, and his dad became a bit of a drifter... Anyway, he and Carol were a little older than us, but they started dating—"

"Ahem!" My mom cleared her throat loudly and darted her eyes toward their eldest sibling—their brother Jackson, who was passing through on his way to the kitchen.

"Looks like quite the coffee klatch!" he teased as he passed.

Ginny's eyes widened. "Right." She lowered her voice to a whisper. "Carol had been dating Jackson when Bud came to town."

My mom nodded solemnly. "Broke Jackson's heart."

"Oh, that was Carol?" said Callie incredulously. She was always a little out of the gossip, being so much younger than her sisters. "I so clearly remember him being upset about that breakup, and I wasn't even *Téa's* age when it happened."

Ginny waved dismissively. "Please! It was for the best. Everyone ended up happy in the end and honestly, what would we have done without Suzie?" As I mentioned, Jackson's wife Suzie's baked goods are the backbone of our family farm stand's offerings. We all paused for a second to imagine the stand without Suzie and couldn't.

Ginny continued. "Anyway, Bud's dad was a waste. Worked part time at the gas station or something. Ended up drowning when he was out trying to fish. The Tanseys, Carol's parents, really took in Bud and even his mom. They basically saved him; Bud was a little off the rails for a while, remember? Then he and Carol got married really young, like at eighteen, and they've been together ever since. They have four kids and have become a strong part of the community, very charitable, and always volunteering for everything. No drama there."

My mom nodded and Callie joked, "Why did all the interesting stuff happen before I was old enough to get it?"

I knew what she meant but had to keep my mouth shut or they'd stop talking.

Callie scrunched up her forehead. "Wait, I do remember one thing! What was it about Bud Slater's dad again? With the fishing? I remember something more about that...?"

Ginny and my mom exchanged a glance. My mom shook her head a tiny bit, but Ginny waved her off. "It's fine. It's old news." She turned to Callie and me and said matter-of-factly, "What happened was, he stole your other grandfather's wooden fishing boat and grounded it on a shoal in Nantucket Sound and it sank. Old Man Slater was drunk and died. The boat was a total loss."

"The boat was hand-built by your dad's dad," added

my mother, her eyes flashing with anger on behalf of her father-in-law. "His main means of livelihood back then."

"Wow," I breathed. "Poor Grandpa Bowers."

"And your grandpa was such a nice man," said my mom, shaking her head. "He built a new boat and got back on his feet—tons of people helped him. But Bud was ashamed, and a lot of people turned against him for that, even though it wasn't his fault."

"Small towns!" said Callie, shaking her head. "Gotta get out!" Ginny singsonged. She half stood and started collecting the sisters' plates; my gold mine was about to leave.

"Wait! I have another family to ask you about," I implored.

Ginny sat back down with the pile of plates balanced on her blue jean–clad knee. "Who?"

"The..." Should I go for the Blooms or the Frankels? I knew I'd only have one chance before my mom insisted that Ginny stop gossiping. "Um...the Blooms? Do you guys know them?"

Ginny squinted. "The name rings a bell. Summer people?"

I started to shake my head "no," but my mom interrupted.

"Originally, I think. They're nice. A little kooky." She stood up and began picking up glasses and stray napkins.

Originally summer people? That was weird. I'd never thought of that before. I'd just assumed that Ziggy's family had been local here for generations, based on things she'd said in the past. I guess, maybe they had. Just not in the way I was thinking.

Callie didn't know them either. I gathered up an hors d'oeuvre platter and followed them into the kitchen. "Yeah, their daughter is my friend. They're hippies, but someone just told me the grandparents are loaded and live on Brookfield Lane."

Ginny put the plates on the counter and put her hand on her hip, furrowing her brow. "Oh, now wait a minute. *Bloom?* Big white house? Black shutters? First one on the left?"

I felt my stomach flip. "Yes?"

"That's right. I dropped off a catering order there a couple of summers ago. Older couple. Very formal. Loaded. From Brookline." Ginny nodded appreciatively.

"But are they related to Ziggy?" I asked my mom.

"I have no idea, sweetheart. That's enough gossip for one child for one night. Now, please go check on the kids. Who knows what they're into now?"

My mind was reeling with all this adult backstory. I grabbed two of Suzie's famous "kitchen sink" cookies (chocolate chips, marshmallows, potato chips, and smashed pretzels...everything but the kitchen sink, in a sugar cookie) and chomped them down as I headed out to the backyard to check on the kids. They were in the garage and had, of course, gotten into some house paint. They were ostensibly trying to paint a sign they "needed" for their fort, but they had tracked through the paint drippings, and it was all over the stone floor of the garage. I quickly cleaned their hands and booted them out to get dessert inside, and then I scrubbed the floor with some turpentine and steel wool I found on the workbench. It wasn't a fancy garage, so the cleanup didn't have to be perfect. I just didn't want my mom to find out there'd been mischief while I was supposed to be watching the kids. I'd never get another scrap of gossip out of her again!

As I neatened everything up and turned off the garage lights, I thought about Bud Slater. It was kind of a sad story, especially about his dad. He must have been so embarrassed. I wondered if Bud Slater was a nice man. I guess that kind of childhood could make you either really nice or really mean. Either way, I was about to find out.

7

Poolies

Bud Slater was not a large man. His shoulders were broad, and his waist tapered into a perfect V. His limbs were long and powerful, and his skin was tanned a burnished walnut. But he gave the impression of size with a booming voice that could cut through chatter and mesmerizing light blue eyes, both of which he used to incredible effect to charm, cajole, or reprimand, as needed. He fascinated me, now that I knew his backstory, and the day of the Junior Lifeguards pool test was the perfect time to observe him, since he was running it.

"Listen up, people! I want thirteen- and fourteen-year-olds to wait on the lower bleachers here, 'cause you are up next. And fifteen and up, down here now because... you're up!"

Dozens of kids shuffled around, glad to have direction but now more obviously nervous, since the time had come to be evaluated.

"Where's Ziggy?" Piper asked for the third or fourth time this morning as we shuffled down to the bottom row of bleachers. By unspoken agreement, we'd still not discussed what Selena had told us on Brookfield Lane the other day. I was bursting to share the information I'd learned from my family and from Google, but it felt kind of sleazy just knowing it, so I kept it to myself for now. I was sure I'd tell Piper at some point. I think I was just embarrassed by how I'd come by the information. Googling and gossiping aren't charitable habits, even though they are fun in the moment.

"Ziggy's always late—except for school. So, what did you expect?" I said.

Ziggy had told Piper at school yesterday that she'd be here this morning. I was curious to know how she'd gotten Mrs. Lisa to do a 180-degree turn and let her try out.

Most crucially, though, the person I was most interested in seeing had not yet appeared either. Maybe Hayden Jones had gone back to his divorced parents in Palm Beach, Florida. Who knew?

Selena was here, though, mute with fear and pale, in a brand new, navy blue Speedo racing bathing suit that was so plain Jane, utilitarian, and un-her. Piper and I had laughed at her in the locker room when she'd come out in it.

Selena's temper could be sharp. "Do you think I like this, this, this...travesty?!" she spat, gesturing at the suit. She held her palms out at us. "Don't speak to me. I hate everyone, and I don't even want to talk until this is finished, understand? Just ignore me like I am not even here!" Her eyes flashed angrily as she pulled her hair into a tight ponytail, another first.

Piper and I had exchanged an amused look, but we took Selena at her word and had ignored her since.

Now Mr. Slater's voice stabbed through the chatter in the echoing room. "Quiet, please! We're going to start in heats of five, going from oldest to youngest. Please listen for your age group to be called. The coaches will write your last name on your left arm in grease pencil. Do not wipe it off. This is how we will keep track of you."

"You're going to do one length of the pool in freestyle, then one lap back in the stroke of your choice. Anything. If you're a great doggie paddler, then by all means, doggie paddle." Bud Slater grinned, and the outer corners of his eyes folded into spectacular fans of wrinkles that encompassed his entire cheeks. (He was nice, I decided. You couldn't have that many smile wrinkles and be mean.)

I made a mental note to do my fabulous butterfly for my second lap. That would wow him!

Slater continued. "You will notice that we are starting in the deep end," he said. "When you finish lap two, the coach will drop two rings to the bottom of the pool. You must swim down and pick them up from the floor of the pool as quickly as possible. Deposit them at the side of the pool. Then you will do a three-minute timed tread. When you are told that you have finished, you may exit the pool and wait to see if you have passed. If you have passed, I will give you an ocean-test release form for your parents to sign, and you are invited to take the ocean test tomorrow. If not, then thank you, good luck, and we'll see you next year."

"I'm *so* glad we don't have to go first," said Piper quietly near my ear. Then, "Do you see Luke?" she asked yet again, but I shook my head as I automatically looked for Hayden and did not find him. Piper's heels bobbed nervously up and down on the tile floor.

"Pipe, you're making me nervous," I admitted. Piper looked at me in shock.

"*You?* Nervous about swimming? You've got to be kidding me! You're so calm, I feel like you're a million miles away!"

Well, I wasn't nervous, but I was a bit distracted, I had to admit. I'd run into Coach Randall on my way in, and she'd very nicely pulled me into her office to wish me luck and remind me that my spot on the team was there for the taking whenever I wanted it back. I thanked her, but it had rattled me a little, making me wonder if I was choosing the right path. Right as I was leaving, Bud Slater popped his head in the door.

"We'll leave right after?" he asked Coach Randall.

"How long do you think it'll take on a Saturday?" she asked.

"'Bout an hour. We should be fine. No traffic at that hour."

"Great. I'll pick up some sandwiches for us."

Slater had nodded and ducked out, and I'd followed right after. It was funny that he and Coach Randall were friends, since it seemed like they'd be competing for the same kids for their programs each summer. I briefly wondered where they were off to, but I was too distracted by the test to focus on it.

Now, the oldest kids finished their trials and Bud called our age group. There were about twenty-five kids in my group, compared to the fifteen or so in the oldest group. Unfortunately for Piper, she had to go in the first heat. Selena and I would go in the next.

She left her towel with me, and I could see her hands shaking.

"It's going to be fine," I tried to comfort her, but it was too little too late, and I felt bad. I'd basically made her do this, after all, and I knew I'd ace the test no problemo, so at least I didn't have to worry about that. I wasn't being a very supportive friend this morning.

"You'll do great," added Selena.

"Mm-hmm," nodded Piper, her eyes far away and distracted. Again, she glanced up at the bleachers. Suddenly, her face turned bright red, and she looked at me with panic in her eyes.

I scanned the crowd until I spied Luke. He was giving Piper the thumbs up.

"I think he likes you," Selena said generously.

I was surprised to feel a twinge of jealousy at Selena's words. Automatically, I scanned the bleachers again; no Hayden. Was I relieved or let down by his absence? I honestly couldn't say.

"Oh stop, Selena! He does not!" Piper now looked pale, like she might faint. She gulped and glanced back at the pool again. "I can't believe he's going to be watching me," she whimpered.

"You'll do awesome! Don't worry!" I said, rising above my petty feelings for the moment. "Just breathe and stay focused on your swimming. Pretend there is no one here but you and the water. That's what I always do. And don't back down from a challenge, remember?"

"I wish I'd worn my rash guard," said Piper plaintively, as she curved her shoulders in and folded her arms in front of her chest.

Selena snapped, "Just get out there and swim! Forget the boys. Make *yourself* proud!" Her eyes flashed and Piper's eyebrows shot up in surprise. But funnily enough, it was just what she needed to hear. She nodded and walked to her position.

Piper took a deep breath and stepped nervously onto the starting block, still trying to cover herself modestly with her crossed arms. She flinched in surprise when one of the lifeguards grabbed her arm and asked her name, but she stood patiently—her pent up energy apparent but contained, like a horse being shod—as the lifeguard scrawled *Janssens* on her upper arm.

I watched as Piper shook out her arms and legs, and knew she was doing it because she'd watched me do it so many times before races. I had to smile. It would be scary to do this if it was your first time. Poor thing.

The whistle sounded and Piper burst off her block and began pulling with big, even strokes, freestyling to the end of the pool. Her breathing was sloppy, but she reached the end of the pool so quickly and turned back, swimming the breaststroke this time. I was impressed. I'd known Piper was strong, but I hadn't realized quite *how* strong. She was half a length ahead of the rest of her heat. I glanced across the pool and saw Coach Randall sidle up next to Bud Slater. Slater said something and Randall nodded, both of them watching Piper intently. I felt a warm flush of...pride? *Jealousy?* I was alarmed at the idea that it could be the latter.

When Piper's wet hand slapped the smooth, curved end of the pool, Bud Slater himself was there to drop her diving rings. Piper took a deep breath, and porpoised down ten feet to the bottom, wiggling her legs and abdomen like an Olympian. *Where the heck did she learn that?* I thought. When both rings were up, she caught her breath as she treaded water. Then Slater nodded at her to signal she was finished, and as she heaved herself up out of the pool, he gave her a huge smile. "Very nice, Miss Janssens," I heard Slater say. "I knew your grandfather. Lovely guy."

Piper smiled back and nodded. I wondered if he would say anything about *my* grandfather. Unlikely.

I stood with a towel open and ready for Piper. She came rushing over to Selena and me with a huge grin. "How'd I do? What did you think? Was I okay?"

I felt myself hesitate for a split second, my shock at her skill still leaving me tongue-tied, but then I exploded in effusive compliments to make up for it. "Oh my God! You were amazing, Piper! Amazing! Even Coach Randall was watching you! She's going to ask you to try out for the team, I bet. She had that recruiting glimmer in her eye! Wow!" I smiled as widely as possible, but something in my heart was clenching and I hated myself for it. *What was wrong with me? Couldn't I be happy for the success of my best friend?*

Selena hugged Piper and planted a giant kiss on her cheek, and then she returned to her marble statue stare, the poor thing. I wondered if she was praying; the Diazes are pretty religious.

Piper grinned maniacally, obviously relieved at being finished and also a little bit proud. She then scanned the bleachers again. I could see all of her limbs were shaking, and I reached over to rub her arm briskly.

But Selena's and my group was up, and I had to get to my block. This was going to be easy breezy. I smiled and stepped into place, totally relaxed. I'd raced from this block millions of times. I pulled my goggles down over my eyes and shook out my arms and legs, nodding at Selena, two blocks over. People grabbed our right arms and penned our names on them.

Suddenly, Bud Slater called from the right side of the pool, his voice booming.

"No goggles!" he yelled.

Everyone went quiet and turned and looked, and suddenly, I realized he was talking to me. I was mortified. Quickly, I ripped them from my eyes and tossed them to Piper, who caught them neatly between her two palms, nodding at me.

"Lifeguards don't have time for goggles when they're making saves! Use your head, girl!" continued Slater.

But my embarrassment quickly turned to anger. *Was I really leaving Coach Randall to be bossed around by this barking guy all summer?* I couldn't believe I'd thought he was nice before! I didn't care what his backstory was. The guy was a jerk!

But then the whistle sounded and regardless of what my brain was thinking, my body was trained to go at that cue. I sliced through the water, porpoised, and then swam like a great white shark was chasing me. Even doing the butterfly on lap two, I beat the other kids in my heat by an entire pool length (sorry, Selena), and was at the end, ready to dive, before a lifeguard was even there with the rings. But when the guy tossed me the rings, I couldn't find them on my first pass. As my embarrassment grew, I came up for air, spotted the rings from above, and dove again. I managed to grab one but couldn't locate the other, and I came back up for a second time, totally frustrated. *Come on, Jenna!* I scolded myself. *For God's sake, this is your home pool. Get it together!*

I dove for a third time and scratched around on the bottom of the pool. The water pressure made my ears throb while my eyes burned from the chlorine. Just as I was about to give up again, I located the second ring and grabbed it. With searing lungs, I shot to the surface, and emerged, gasping, to see Bud Slater staring down at me. Furious, I treaded vigorously for my three minutes, until Slater signaled that I could come out.

"Nice stroke, Poolie, but you're gonna have to toughen up if you want to be an ocean guard one day," said Bud as I swung myself out of the pool in an angry but still graceful arc.

Oh my God, I failed, was all I could think. And also, *Your dad crashed my grandpa's boat, you jerk!* But I said nothing and just walked away.

Piper was waiting for me with my towel "Oh, Jenna," sighed Piper. "You are such a talented swimmer. Nice job!"

Selena was smiling for the first time all morning. "You are a superstar swimmer!" she cried proudly, hugging me around the neck. She had finished before me and was already dried off in her towel.

I blotted my stinging eyes with my towel. I had never realized how much I depended on my goggles. There was no way I could be a lifeguard if I couldn't see underwater.

"Thanks, but I'm not doing this. Today was a waste of my time," I said curtly. I'd decided, then and there, that I wasn't going to give Slater the satisfaction of failing me. He'd probably enjoy failing a Bowers, assuming he knew who I was.

Instead, I'd just quit while I was ahead. Coach Randall had just told me she'd love to have me back, hadn't she? "I'll see you guys later," I said, and began to walk to the locker room.

Piper looked at me, stricken. "Wait, *what*? You can't leave! Are you nuts? You're the one who made me do this!" She grabbed my arm to pull me back.

"Then you leave too," I said, shrugging off her hand. "You'll get your job back. I'll do swim team."

"I...I..." Piper stammered. She didn't know what to say. "But... I did a good job!"

I blinked. "So?" I was daring her to admit that I hadn't done a good job.

Piper set her jaw. "So, I don't walk away from a challenge."

"That's *my* line." I stared at Piper for a second. Neither one of us blinked.

"Jenna," said Selena quietly. She touched me on the arm, and I flinched.

I was annoyed that I'd ever gotten any of us involved in this whole thing. If I even passed this test—never mind the ocean test—and did Junior Lifeguards, it would probably *ruin* my summer hanging around that jerky Bud Slater. But if I didn't, then I'd have to go back on everything I'd said to my parents and to Coach Randall and to all my best friends.

It was like swimming out to the raft that was anchored at the bay beach when I was little: Sometimes I got just past halfway out and changed my mind, but I had to keep going because it was too far to go back without a rest. *Had I gone so far that I had to keep going with this?*

"Jen?" repeated Selena.

"What?" I replied finally, but in a cranky voice.

Selena was unaffected by my grumpiness. "Let's all do it together, if we pass, I mean. It will be so much more fun that way. If I can't go away to acting camp, at least we can all be together. Come on. We *need* you, chica!" She made her eyes all big and round and innocent, like she does when she forgets her homework and doesn't want the teacher to yell at her.

"You guys don't need me," I said, turning away again. But as I did, something caught my eye: Hayden. He had appeared out of nowhere and was now standing with a group of the older guys on the bleachers. Though his back was to me, I could see that he was telling a funny story, and it was very amusing to the little crowd; he was clearly the life of the party. Watching him, I felt my face growing warm. He turned to the side and his face was so gorgeous and grown-up—ruddy cheeks, tan skin, thick, dark eyebrows and eyelashes, huge brown eyes, high cheekbones—he made Luke Slater look like a child.

Was he sketchy, though, or was I imagining it? And why hadn't he taken the test? He was wearing a bathing suit and tee shirt, but he was bone-dry.

"Jenna," Piper was impatient now. I could hear it in her voice, and I turned my body back toward her and Selena but did not take my eyes off Hayden.

Piper continued. "Stop feeling sorry for yourself about the stupid ring diving. You can't be great at everything. Stay here and see this through with us. Then we can be lifeguards together when we're sixteen. Think how fun that would be! Think how much money we'll make! Think of the cute guys!" Now the shoe was on the other foot, and Piper was using all of my lines to convince me. "Think of how great it will look on your college apps!"

All of a sudden, Piper stopped. She thought I wasn't listening to anything she was saying.

"Jenna?"

"Hmmm?"

Piper followed my gaze and then grinned. "You'll do it, right?"

I sighed. "Do what?"

"Jenna!" Piper punched me playfully in the arm.

I rubbed my arm thoughtfully, a half smile on my face. "Maybe."

"Yay!" squealed Selena, and she and Piper high-fived.

The truth was, I was sure I'd failed. I could just feel it in my bones. Hot guy or no hot guy, I might not be doing Junior Lifeguards after all. And it wasn't up to me at all.

Just then, we were interrupted by a casual, "Hi everyone!"

Ziggy had arrived.

Quitter

"Zigs!" cried Piper. They hugged.

"Wait, are you trying out?" I asked. I looked up at the big clock on the wall; she was forty-five minutes late!

"I'm here, aren't I?" Ziggy giggled, showing no sense of urgency or distress at her tardiness. I would have been embarrassed if I were her, but this thought flitted through my mind right then: maybe if your family is rich (whether or not it shows), you don't need to try as hard for things you want.

But just as quickly, I swallowed the idea and scolded myself for thinking mean thoughts about my friend's secrets.

"So, did your parents say yes?" Selena was asking.

Ziggy gathered her curls into a braid. She shrugged. "You know, my parents and I... Let's just say, they don't know I'm here right now. I don't even have the check or paperwork."

Piper looked at Ziggy anxiously. "Go check in now and tell them you forgot it. I'm sure they'll let you do it anyway. Come back after. I get the sense that Bud Slater doesn't appreciate lateness."

"Really? Okay," said Ziggy, still unworried. "Back in a minute!" She wiggled her fingers at us and sauntered off toward Slater.

I shook my head in wonder as we watched her catch up with him. Punctuality had been demanded of me and my brothers practically from birth (my dad always says, "Five minutes early is on time! On time is late," much to our annoyance). Anything my dad hadn't drilled into me about being on time, Coach Randall had.

"Who are you, young lady, and why are you so late?" we could hear Bud Slater bark as he sized up the pint-sized girl in front of him.

Adults never intimidated Ziggy. She smiled widely up at him. "Hi, I'm Ziggy Bloom, and I'd like to take the swim test today, please. I'm sorry I was late. It was...unavoidable, sir."

The "sir" had been a good idea. I could see Slater's posture soften, and he seemed to calm down. He was obviously a man who liked respect and order. I watched them and felt proud of Ziggy, even as I disliked Slater more. I wondered how my old sitter Molly could have stood being around him for all those years of lifeguard training.

"You can't be late when it comes to saving lives, Miss Bloom. In fact, you should never be late for anything in life. You should always be early."

Ziggy Bloom, who had never been on time for anything

except school (how, I'll never know) grinned heartily and nodded her head. "I agree, sir. Completely. I am sorry."

Bud Slater looked at her quizzically, as if to see if she were putting him on, or if he could trust her. Ziggy smiled charmingly at him, waited patiently, and finally he nodded.

"And your paperwork is all set, I assume?" he said.

Uh-oh. Here it came. I braced myself.

Ziggy smiled still, charmingly. "I was in such a rush, I forgot it at home. I'm so sorry, sir!"

Bud Slater sighed in exasperation and shook his head. "Fine. Go to lane four and wait your turn. You will go last, all by yourself. Don't ever be late again. And get me that paperwork, please." He turned on his heel and walked away.

Ziggy looked up at us with a palms-up shrug and a big grin. Piper gave her an encouraging wave, and Selena gave the thumbs up; I was too annoyed. *Why can some people break rules and get away with it*, I thought, *when the rest of us work hard to do everything right?* Things like this drive me nuts!

When everyone had finished, Ziggy stepped up to lane four, had her name scrawled on her arm, and jumped in the pool for her swim. All in all, her test was a disaster, with Ziggy crashing into the lane dividers and taking multiple trips to find the rings. Ziggy couldn't stop smiling the whole time, though. I don't know if she was nervous or thought it was funny. Either way, I couldn't watch by the end of it; my head was in my hands.

Afterward, Bud Slater ambled over to Ziggy and said something we couldn't hear. Seconds later, Ziggy came to the bleachers to join us.

"Great job, Zigs!" said Piper.

Ziggy rolled her eyes. "I was a disaster! Like a rodeo clown—I did everything wrong!"

"What was it that Slater said to you after?" asked Selena.

Ziggy laughed. "He said," she put on a fake serious,

deep voice to imitate him, "'Well, Miss Bloom, you're not an ace in the water yet, but we can probably help you with that. It's the smile I like. Just be careful not to turn into the class clown, because I don't like that.'"

"What a jerk that guy is!" I said, relieved he hadn't been mean only to me.

Ziggy's smiled faded. "I know. Maybe my mom was right. Yuck. I hate it when that happens!"

"Ugh, me too!" agreed Piper.

"So, Pipe, did ya talk to Luke?" asked Ziggy, changing the subject.

Piper laughed and blushed. "No. I didn't have a chance. But he did give me a thumbs up. I think he's leaving now." We all turned to watch him exit the pool area.

Ziggy nodded. "Probably on duty today." Piper sighed. "Going off to save people. So noble."

Selena, Ziggy, and I laughed.

"How about Hayden?" asked Selena, looking around.

I had been so focused on Ziggy's test that I had

forgotten to keep track of Hayden. When I scanned the bleachers, I saw that he was gone.

But why was Selena wondering?

Bud Slater was now circling the pool with his clipboard, telling the kids who had passed and handing them sheets of paper. It looked like about half of the kids were being invited to the ocean test tomorrow.

After an eternity, Slater reached the four of us. I couldn't even meet his eye.

He went to Piper first.

"Miss Janssens, very nice test today. Please join us tomorrow," Slater said with a nod. Piper nodded back as he handed her a sheet of paper. "This is the ocean test release form. Bring this signed by your guardian or I can't let you swim."

"Thanks!" said Piper, smiling up at him nervously. I

looked away again. Slater was working his way down the row. I would be last.

"Miss Bloom." I watched them with interest; would he be kind or curt, I wondered.

Ziggy sat up straight. "Yes, sir?"

OMG, enough with the brown-nosing, Ziggy, I thought, uncharitably. I suddenly wanted to gag at Ziggy's phoniness.

Slater handed her the release. "Loved the smile. Please bring it back tomorrow."

What? I couldn't believe it! I almost gasped out loud! How had she passed? Ziggy could barely swim! *What was going on here?*

"Yes!" said Ziggy, and she pumped her fist in the air.

"On time—not a minute late. And with both releases signed, and the check," Slater added, a serious look on his face.

"Right. Sorry," Ziggy ducked her head, and her smile faded.

"Diaz?" Slater glanced at Selena's arm.

"Yes?" Selena looked up and batted her eyes innocently at Slater.

But he was immune to her charms. "I'm accepting you conditionally. I'd like you to brush up on your strokes. We're having a few clinics here at the pool the next few Wednesdays. I'd like to see you there if you're serious about our program, okay?"

"I..." Selena stammered. She barely wanted to do Junior Lifeguards, and now this.

Slater waved her off. "Totally up to you. If you want to participate. See you tomorrow, if so." He handed her the ocean test release.

And now it was my turn.

"Last but not least, Miss..." Bud searched his clipboard, lifting one page, then looking back at the previous one again.

"Bowers!" I barked, finally, showing him my arm. Was this a joke or did he really not know who I was?

"Right! Bowers! Please join us tomorrow as an alternate,"

he said, offering me the handout. "And no goggles!" he added with a wink, and then he turned to walk away.

"What's an alternate?" I called after him, the paper hanging limply in my hand. I could feel my face suddenly flame red.

Slater turned back and looked at me. "I can't guarantee you a spot in your age group. But if someone doesn't pass tomorrow and you do, then it's yours."

I gulped. "You mean I should hope one of my friends fails so I can be in if I pass?"

"That's the idea," he shrugged, and then he just walked away.

I was mortified.

Piper's jaw dropped in surprise.

"What the...?" Ziggy began.

"Hey!" Selena called after him.

But I jumped up and ran in the opposite direction, totally disregarding the no running rule. I balled the paper up and tossed it backwards over my shoulder as I ran. In the locker room, I grabbed my bag without even changing, and then pushed through the crowd and ran out.

I jumped on my bike in my bathing suit, with shaking legs and tears streaming down my face, and pedaled home as fast as my legs could take me. Bud Slater had it out to humiliate me. I wasn't going to give him a chance to do it again.

⁓

"Jenna?"

Even with two pillows over my head, I could hear my friends enter my house.

I'd known they would come.

I was done with the crying (I really *really* hate to cry) and was now just moping in my bed with my cat, Seal. She's all shiny black, so she looks like a seal, but I was going through a big Naval Academy fascination when I got her two years ago, so her name is really S.E.A.L. Dorky, I know.

"Jen?" someone called.

I waited an extra second, then I lifted the pillows and yelled, "What?" in an angry voice.

The door opened, and Selena, Ziggy, and Piper crammed into my small room.

I stared down at them from my loft bed. "Hi," said Piper softly.

The three of them jostled awkwardly, as if they had been rehearsing who was going to say what but now couldn't start.

I flipped onto my back to stare at the ceiling. "Oh, just get on with it," I said, waving my hand.

Piper began. "Jenna, we feel so bad that you were the one who got us all to try out and then, well..."

"I failed?" I said in an angry voice.

Selena climbed up my ladder. "You didn't fail, mi amor," she said, rubbing my foot over the covers. "You were the best swimmer there. We were so proud of you!"

"Jenna, we think Slater was trying to teach you a lesson," said Piper.

I could hear her settle into my swivel desk chair underneath me and begin spinning from side to side, just as a loud crunch indicated that Ziggy had flopped into my bean bag chair.

"What? Why would that be? He doesn't even know me!" I said. I turned onto my side and propped my head up on my hand. I had to admit, I'd been mulling it all over in my head, and I knew it had to be something. I mean, I'd swam really well! It was just the diving part that got me. It wasn't fail-worthy, really.

"Well, think of this: It was something different for everyone. Piper, he lets in. Done!" Selena said, beginning to count us off on her fingers. "Me, he says I'm in, but I need swim lessons. Yuck on that, by the way. And Ziggy, she needs two releases signed, has to keep smiling, can't be late."

"So?" I said, rolling my eyes.

"And you, he makes an alternate!" concluded Selena. "This is just him playing games with your head! He probably thought you were too good, so he wanted to take you down a peg. That's what we think."

"It's the only possible explanation," said Piper from underneath my loft.

"Let me get this straight: He failed me because I'm too good?" I laughed a fake bitter laugh. "Right. That's a good one." I debated telling them the family history, but I worried that if I started by sharing one family's secrets, they'd all come tumbling out, like a ball of yarn unraveling.

There was a pause.

"He made you an alternate because he thought you were cocky," said Piper, matter-of-factly.

The room went dead silent. I looked at Selena; she was aghast at what Piper had said, but not surprised.

My face burned red. "Was I?" I asked quietly.

Selena tipped her head from side to side, "A tiny bit. But totally natural anyway. You're a great swimmer. It wasn't something other people would have noticed."

I groaned, embarrassed now.

Suddenly, Ziggy popped up on the ladder next to Selena. "I didn't see it that way at all, just for the record. And you can have my spot, Jenna. I can't use it anyway."

"Thanks, Ziggy, but that's beside the point," I said. "And you didn't see me take the test, by the way. It was bad."

"I doubt it was as bad as you think." Ziggy looked at me sadly and climbed back down. *Crunch* went the beanbag again.

"Jenna, he didn't *fail* you!" said Piper, punching the mattress from underneath as she said "fail." The punch made a muffled *boom* sound, and Seal jumped up from my bed, bounded down the ladder and out the door.

"Hey!" I laughed in spite of myself, and Piper did it again.

"Stop!" I laughed.

Piper now began to pound the underside of my bed.

"Stop! For real!" I yelled, but I was still laughing. "I'll only stop if you say you're coming to the ocean test tomorrow!" yelled Piper.

"No! No way!" I cried.

"Is Jenna Bowers a quitter?" yelled Piper. *Pound, pound, pound!* "Does she back down from a challenge?"

I hesitated, even though the pounding was driving me nuts.

Was I a quitter? Of course not! But would it actually qualify as quitting if I didn't go to the test as an alternate? And what if I passed? Was I signing on to be Bud Slater's scapegoat for the rest of the summer?

"You need to see this through!" Piper called. "Tell me you're doing it! My hand is getting sore!"

I paused again.

"Hayden will be there!" cried Selena, a grin on her face. I looked quickly at her. She wasn't playing fair!

"How do you know?" I asked nervously. "Did you speak to him?"

"Trust me," said Selena, in a kind of annoying know-it-all way.

"Jenna!" wailed Piper. "Come on!"

"Oh, fine, whatever!" I conceded finally. At the very least, I wasn't going to just hand Hayden over to Selena without trying.

The pounding stopped. "Thank goodness!" moaned Piper.

I hung over the railing of the bed and looked at her from upside down. She was cradling her fist, which was all red.

"You scared my cat," I accused.

Piper grinned wickedly. "It was worth it."

"And for the record," I declared, coming back up and looking at Selena. "I don't like Hayden Jones."

Selena patted my foot "Sure you don't, baby. Whatever you say."

"I'm only doing it tomorrow because I'm not a quitter. I'll see it through. And then when Slater *fails* me tomorrow, you guys don't get to bug me anymore. I'll go back on swim team, and we'll forget this ever happened. Except that you'll all become lifeguards and I won't. Okay?"

"Oh, here we go again!" wailed Piper.

"No. That's all." I said. "Just agree."

"Okay, fine, whatever, we agree. Now, what do you have to eat around here?" asked Ziggy, standing.

"Thanks, you guys," I said. "I love my friends."

"We love you too, Jenny," said Piper, teasing me with the name I hate most of all. (Actually, I have nothing against the name itself, but people always think that's my name when I introduce myself, and I can't stand it.)

"Don't push your luck!" I warned, as I climbed down the ladder.

"Here," said Piper, handing me the form Slater had given me. They'd smoothed it out and it looked pretty good; like it had gotten accidentally crunched in my backpack, not intentionally smushed and tossed on the ground.

"Thanks," I sighed as I looked at it. It actually didn't say anything about being an alternate on it. It looked exactly like the forms he'd given everyone else. Maybe there was some truth to what my friends were thinking.

"I think we have some banana crunch muffins from the stand," I said, suddenly starving. Banana crunch muffins were rare treats (too labor-intensive for regular rotation) that my aunt Suzie made to sell at the family farm stand. My mom always pinched a six-pack to bring home for me because I love them so much. Ziggy would be happy because Suzie makes them with all organic ingredients, which has absolutely nothing to do with why I love them!

"By the way, we did see Hayden after, and he asked where you were," said Ziggy.

"Really?! I mean, oh. Huh." I tried to play it cool as I pulled on my sweatpants. "There is definitely something sketchy there, because he did not take that test today."

My friends all looked at each other in surprise. I shrugged. "I'm just saying."

"He said he'd see us at the ocean test tomorrow, though," said Piper.

We bustled out of my room and headed toward the kitchen.

"Weird," said Selena. But when I looked at her face, she actually looked more impressed than confused.

"Very," I agreed, but her expression would stay with me for the rest of the day.

9

The Ocean Test

It was fitting that Sunday morning dawned gray and chilly, spitting rain in sharp little needles. It matched my mood.

I had tossed and turned all night thinking about the pool test, Junior Lifeguards, Bud Slater, his family history, Hayden Jones, my friends, and our summer. One conclusion I'd reached was that the ocean test was a formality. Slater had already made his mind up about me; I just couldn't guess whether I would be in or out.

Another conclusion I'd reached was that Selena would

get Hayden if she really wanted him. What I couldn't decide was whether I'd put up a fight for him along the way.

Finally, I'd concluded that, despite my misgivings about Slater and the other participants, I really *wanted* to do Junior Lifeguards this summer. I wanted to learn all that interesting stuff. I wanted to sit up in that stand. I wanted to save people and have them think I was a hero like Molly. I wanted it all.

At the ocean test at Lookout Beach this morning, there were about half as many kids as yesterday, though I wasn't sure if that was because of who qualified or because of the weather. Probably a bit of both. I stuck my bike in the rack and jogged over to the beach pavilion where a crowd of kids had gathered under the roof. Most of them were kids I knew from school or town in general, though there were a bunch who were unrecognizable to me—summer kids and some kids from other nearby towns.

Selena, Piper, and Ziggy weren't here yet, but Bud and Luke Slater were. And so was Hayden Jones. I took a deep breath. I wanted to go say hi to Hayden, but I was shy; I knew I should turn in my forms first anyway. Clearly, Bud Slater was a stickler for punctuality, so I might as well show him I was early.

I wound my way through the group to the pavilion railing where Slater stood with some other town lifeguards.

"Mr. Slater?" I began.

He turned. "Ms. Bowers. Nice to see you here bright and early this beautiful morning." His tone was friendly, but he wasn't smiling so I didn't smile either. I couldn't help but wonder if his knowing my name was a good thing or a bad thing.

I held my release form out toward him. "Here is my paperwork."

He glanced at it and nodded, then handed it to another lifeguard who had a growing pile of papers. "Looking forward to seeing what you've got today."

Was this a challenge?

"I'm a pretty good ocean swimmer," I said evenly.

Slater paused for a second, looking out at the water. Then he said, "I don't doubt that. I'm mostly interested in attitude."

Now it was my turn to hesitate. After a second or two, I said, "I think you'll find I have a very good attitude."

He turned to me and smiled at last. "Good. I'm looking forward to it."

And suddenly, "Well, well, well, looky who's here!"

I turned at the sound of the gravelly deep voice arriving behind me.

Hayden!

I blushed and grinned all at the same time. *Real suave, Bowers.* I could feel Slater watching me, and that made me blush more. When I stole a glance at him, he seemed to be stifling a laugh, which was annoying to me.

"Mr. Jones," said Slater, putting his hand out for a shake.

Hayden reached out and shook Slater's hand. "Better," said Slater. "You're getting the hang of it."

Hayden rolled his eyes, then he turned to me and said, "Let's check out *your* handshake, Jenna Bowers!"

I put out my hand and gave him a strong shake, just like my dad always coaches us to. Hayden faked like I'd hurt him and howled and shook his hand after I let go. I grinned like an idiot because just shaking his hand had sent a jolt of happy electricity up my arm. When I glanced at Slater, I could see him looking at me in a different way—his head was tipped back a bit and his eyes narrowed, like he was appraising me. Then he nodded and smiled.

"Nice work, Bowers. Keep this guy in line for me, all right?" And Slater gave me a clap on the back and turned back to talk to the other lifeguards.

Oookay, I thought. *That was weird.*

Hayden and I walked away from the railing, and began to chat, but inside my mind was reeling with questions. Why did Slater even like Hayden? And why did it seem like just because Hayden and I were friendly, Slater suddenly liked me a little more?

"So, when are we getting our ice cream?" asked Hayden.

I blushed again. He'd remembered!

"Oh! Um. How about after we pass the test? We can celebrate?" Not that I had high hopes.

Now it was Hayden's turn to blush. "Right. Okay. Yeah. When we pass." He nodded vigorously.

Oh, gosh. I suddenly realized that I am an idiot! I was *sure* something fishy was going on in terms of his qualifications. Maybe Slater wasn't making him swim for a reason. Was he on, like, the Junior Olympic Swim Team or something? I itched to google all of a sudden!

"Or if we fail the test, we can commiserate over an ice cream! Either way," I said, kind of testing him.

Hayden looked away and nodded. "Great."

"So, wait, have you done Junior Lifeguards before?" I asked, my confusion apparent in my voice.

Hayden shook his head and looked out at the ocean. "Nope. Never spent the summer at the beach before."

I could feel my eyebrows knit together in confusion. "So...how do you know Mr. Slater then?"

"Oh, we're old family friends," Hayden spoke quickly.

"He and my dad went to boarding school together back in the day."

Aha! Boarding school! Another piece of backstory that fit into what I'd heard. Summer kids went to boarding school; locals really didn't. "Oh. Okay. Cool. He seems…"

Right as I was fibbing and saying "nice," Hayden said "tough" and we both laughed.

"He's both," said Hayden, nodding.

"I guess I can see that," I said.

"Guys!" We were interrupted by Piper, calling out from her grandmother's pickup truck. I waved and she said goodbye to Bett and hopped out of the truck, jogging over to us.

"So, it's on?" she asked, slightly out of breath.

I laughed. "Yeah. Were you hoping it would be canceled?"

"Well…*yeah*! The weather's awful!"

"Oh, Piper," I shook my head.

"The ocean never takes a day off!" joked Hayden.

"How would you know, landlubber?" I teased and elbowed him in the side. He cried "OW!" and fake-clutched his side, like I'd hurt him for real. I giggled.

Piper looked at us flirting and grinned knowingly at me. I raised my eyebrows in acknowledgment of her grin and grinned back.

"Anyway, what about hurricanes?" said Piper, wrapping herself in her towel and shivering. "The ocean's closed on those days."

"True, but it's not because it's taking the day off. It's because it's too busy to host anyone."

Piper waved her hand. The joke had gone too far, and she was distracted, anyway. She turned to watch the water. After a second, she said, "It *is* pretty choppy out there. And I'm sure it's cold."

I looked with her and nodded. "The good thing about lifeguarding is that not many people go in when it's like this." I pictured Molly up on her stand on a crummy day, huddled inside her thick hoodie, under a beach towel and a big beach umbrella that wedged into a clamp on the side of the ladder. Besides looking cold, she'd looked bored. "Anyway, you know what my dad always says! You have to have the bad days..."

"...to appreciate the good!" chimed Piper.

My dad had lots of sayings, and my friends knew them all. We laughed and shook our heads in affectionate annoyance at my good old dad. I glanced at Hayden and realized he was looking at us oddly.

"Does your dad hang out with you guys a lot? Like, your friends can quote him?" he asked incredulously.

I was embarrassed suddenly. Duh! I am clueless. Obviously it's not cool to talk about your parents in front of a boy you like. I had some damage control to do now. "Um. Yes? I know. It's *totally* dorky. We all wish my parents would just scram, you know? They're so annoying and just around all the time at everything. Right, Piper?" I rolled my eyes.

Piper laughed. "Yes, they're around all the time, but I love them, so I don't think it's dorky. And no one else does either."

"Huh," said Hayden, and I wanted to die. But then, "That's cool," he added, looking away.

Oh. Um. Okay?

"People! Listen up! Over here!" It was Bud Slater, doing that ventriloquist act with his foghorn voice again, so that it sounded like he was right inside my head even though he was across the pavilion from me. "It's a beautiful day for a swim in the ocean! Come on down!" he cried.

"It's go time," I whispered, mostly to myself. I looked around the crowd as we surged toward Slater. Selena was just running in, but there was no sign of Ziggy. (Shocker.) Piper, Hayden, and I drew in to where Slater was standing, and Selena came jogging up behind me.

"Hey," she whispered.

"Hey!" I whispered back. I watched carefully to see how she interacted with Hayden, but he didn't seem to care about her arrival. He nodded a casual hello and turned back to focus on Slater. I tried not to smile, but it made me feel really good inside, like maybe Hayden actually liked me better than Selena. It would be a first in my life.

There was a tap on my shoulder, and I turned around to see Ziggy standing there with a huge grin, dwarfed by a down jacket!

"Shalom!" she whispered.

"OMG, Ziggy! You're here! And what are you wearing?!" I had to laugh, but I quickly glanced back at Slater and saw he was waiting for us to settle down before he continued. I made my face go into its best alert-and-focused look (the one I usually save for Latin class).

I saw Slater note Selena and Ziggy's arrivals with a nod and then he continued, "The test today will have two parts. First, you and a partner will swim with a guard out past the break. There you will tread water for five minutes. Next you will swim in a parallel course across the beach, a distance of about three hundred yards, and then swim in, get out, and report back to me. Do not let your partner out of your sight. Do not leave your partner behind. Do not exit the water without him or her. Do not walk away from the water's edge unless they are with you. Is that clear?"

Everyone nodded and looked around.

"Test results will be posted Tuesday afternoon at the rec center. Some acceptances might be conditional. That means you will be asked to take a series of extra swim lessons at the rec center on Wednesdays. You can follow up with me directly to schedule these if that is the case. Otherwise, please do not ask me if you passed today. Understand?"

People murmured their assent, and then Slater directed us into a line of pairs. There was shuffling and maneuvering as everyone counted off to see who their buddy would be. Ziggy elbowed me.

"Who's that?" she asked in a whisper, her eyes locked onto a striking-looking guy off to the side a little. He was very tan, Asian, with streaky, reddish-blond hair, and though he was thin and petite, he was ripped. He was alone, quiet and self-contained, standing in just a pair of board shorts. He did not seem bothered at all by the cold.

"Cute!" replied Piper.

I turned back, a little impressed. I knew who it was because I'd seen an article on him in the *Cape Cod Times* last fall. "It's Jack Lee. Surfing champ. Sponsored by Quicksilver! He goes to Blake." Blake went to the super-genius charter school one town over.

"I hope *he* makes it!" said Ziggy with a giggle.

"You two would look amazing together!" I agreed.

But then I shook my head to clear it of boys and all the related distractions. I needed to focus on Slater now. I had to get this right today. I just had to.

"All right, step forward, and be ready to hand me your release," Slater's voice cut through their chatter. Piper and I stepped into place; we would get to go together. I wasn't sure if this was a good idea strategically, but it did make me feel good to be with Piper.

Piper squeezed my hand and whispered, "I'm glad you came."

"Thanks," I whispered back. I wouldn't actually know if I was glad I came until after the test.

I turned to see if Selena and Ziggy were paired and was surprised to see that Ziggy had slipped back and off to the side and was standing with her arms folded inside her jacket. I tried to catch her attention but Ziggy was looking off toward the horizon. Selena was now right behind us, paired with a girl named April who was in the grade below us at school.

Hayden had disappeared.

I whipped my head left and right and craned my neck to see if he had gone to the back of the line, but he was just plain gone! Mixed emotions surged inside me. I'd wanted him to see me swim well, and I'd wanted to see *him* swim so I could put my mind at ease about some of his possible sketchiness. And most of all, I'd wanted him around, in general, to smile at. But maybe it was less distracting if he wasn't here watching. Maybe it was a good thing if it turned out he had left. Maybe he'd just gone to the bathroom and would be back in a minute!

As I was turning back toward Slater, I spied a figure ambling down the gray, wooden staircase that cut through the dunes beyond the pavilion. The Frankels' dunes.

I squinted. After a moment, I could see that it was a girl, with nut-brown skin and a mane of gorgeous, wild brown curls that lay down her back and bounced, as a unit, when she walked. And despite the cold and occasional spitting rain, she was wearing nothing more than a tiny white bikini, which was electric against her dark skin.

I elbowed Piper who turned to me and then spotted the girl.

"Look! It's one of the Frankels," I whispered.

Piper's jaw dropped. "She's got on a gold belly chain!" she said in amazement.

"Come on!" I said, and I squinted to see if it was true. Sure enough, there it was, glimmering around the girl's waist like a fallen halo.

I turned to catch Selena's eye, but she was resolutely looking the other way, her jaw set. She must've seen the Frankel girl and was pretending not to; maybe she wanted to be sure the girl didn't come join her. Poor Selena. This would be awkward. On the one hand, she was practically an employee of the Frankels'. On the other hand, she was probably this girl's lifeline—the only person she knew here.

Just as the girl reached the edge of the pavilion, Piper and I were up, and Luke had reappeared at the front of the line as our escort, his shock of yellow hair soaked and his wet suit shiny with seawater from his last swim. My stomach flickered nervously with the usual butterflies; this was it! I ditched my towel and anorak on a bench and watched as Piper parted with her towel with great difficulty. Poor Piper. She was so shy in a bathing suit, but she looked totally adorable!

"You look good, don't worry," I said, generously.

Piper looked up at me in surprise, then anxiety furrowed her brow. "Ugh," she said. "But thanks anyway. And why did it have to be Luke who takes us? It's *so* my life. Just watch me make a total fool of myself!"

"Stop that right now!" My voice came out a little more harshly than I wanted, and I could see Piper was taken aback.

"Sorry," I apologized. "It's just that's a really dangerous attitude to have going into this."

Piper took a deep breath. "Right," she said. "Think positive!" And at the last possible second, she reached over to her towel and grabbed her stretched-out pink rash guard and pulled it on.

"Oh!" I was about to protest that a rash guard would be more harm than help in this water, but it was too late. Slater was calling us, and so we set off to greet Luke: bad attitudes, beautiful Frankel sisters, and poor outfit choices temporarily set aside.

"Hello, ladies!" Luke said with a welcoming grin. He crooked his arms and offered one to each of us. Piper couldn't help but smile back, and her blue eyes lit up as she grabbed onto his arm. I felt happy for her as we marched down toward the frothing, cold water.

"Okay, Piper, so I know you're a Janssens," he said. Piper's face burned with pleasure. "I figured out that I know your grandma from yoga, and you look just like her. In a good way." He winked and Piper looked like she was going to swoon.

"And you are a Bowers," he said, turning to me. His tone of voice was totally neutral, so I couldn't read into it.

"Yup," I said, wondering how much he knew of our grandfathers' history together. I didn't want to say anything more.

"And a Tucker on the other side. From the farm stand?" he asked. I glanced at him in surprise. He *had* been researching us!

"Yup," I nodded again.

"Hey, so are we supposed to call you Mr. Slater too?" teased Piper.

I looked at her quizzically. Piper was never bold like

this. Maybe it was because of her nerves. *People on their way to the electric chair were probably really chatty too,* I thought.

"Yes. In fact, I insist that you call me Mr. Slater," he replied with a mischievous grin. "But with good behavior, I might let you earn the privilege of calling me sir."

Piper giggled and I smiled. It was good to see Piper relaxing.

This guy's so warm and friendly, like a trained dolphin, I thought distractedly. *He must take after his mother because Bud Slater is all sharp edges.* Then I shook my head a little; my mind was not in the game. I needed to focus now on the swim: How many strokes would it take to cross the beach? What would my timing be, allowing for the pull of the waves and crosscurrent? How should I pace my breathing, especially if the water was freezing?

Luke stole a sidelong glance at Piper as we approached the water. "Thinkin' about ditchin' the rash guard?" he asked lightly.

Piper pinkened. "Um...no. Why? Should I?"

I thought, *Good call.* Maybe Luke Slater wasn't dolphin-like after all. I held my breath awaiting his reply.

"Might not be the best thing to wear for this because it won't keep you warm and it will drag some, but it's up to you."

We had reached the water. It was freezing. My toes recoiled instinctively.

"I think I'll keep it," said Piper firmly.

Bad idea, I thought.

"Your call," conceded Luke with a shrug and a smile. "Alas, ladies, reluctant as I am to relinquish your lovely arms, I must now do so. It is time to see if you have what it takes...*to be a guard!*" He finished in a self-mocking tone. "C'mon!"

He jumped through the foamy whitewater, light on his feet, his knees raised high with each step, without pause. But Piper and I stalled, looking at each other, and then we followed suit. I received the blow of the icy water by dunking under as quickly as possible. But Piper buckled at the knees as if the wind had been knocked out of her, and I turned to see her fighting against getting wet, her arms held aloft, and each inch of water making her half shriek. Luke turned back and Piper forced a smile onto her face that was more like a grimace. She took huge, gulping breaths as she staggered in. I watched Piper's rash guard balloon above the water as the ocean pushed up the air inside. Piper ineffectually tried to pat it down, but it wouldn't go.

Luke turned back again and waved us on. Then, he began to swim out.

I turned back to face the break where all the waves crashed one after another and had to quickly dive a sizable wave.

When I came up, I was on the far side of the break and Piper was still back by the shore.

"Piper!" I cried over the wind and waves, but she couldn't hear me.

10

Flailing

"Darn it!" I muttered. I turned to look for Luke, but he was already farther out, swimming straight away from us. The waves were crashing one after the other in a long set. I kept losing sight of Piper as the waves rose and fell between us. I felt caught. Should I go back and help Piper get out past the break? Should I stay where I was and hope my presence here was encouragement enough to draw her out? Would Piper even come, or would she just turn back and quit? I really wanted her to join me. I wanted us to be lifeguards together!

Slater's words echoed in my mind. *"Do not let your partner out of your sight. Do not leave your partner behind."* Was this part of the test?

I sighed hard and slapped the water, and then I turned to time my return to Piper so I could get a ride in from a wave. But just as I was about to swim in, she seemed to rally and with strong, short strokes, she swam out toward me, ducking the occasional wave, until she reached my side about 30 yards out. I nodded at her and said, "Good job," and she nodded back, one short, quick nod. Neither of us could really speak right now. We swam further out to where Luke had just stopped; he had finally turned back to look for us. He waved as we approached, and the whiteness of his smile glowed through the salty spray of the water.

When we reached him, Luke and I floated, treading water. Piper floated too, sort of, but her arms and legs were jerking nervously as they treaded, like a marionette operated by a three-year-old. Her rash guard was stretched out and pooled loosely in front of her, and I could see the wet weight of it pulling on her shoulders, trapping the cold against her skin. Useless, just as Luke had implied. And now it was too late to do anything about it.

Obviously, we couldn't really chat, but Luke called, "Nice job, you two!" and I nodded briefly. Like usual, I sang a song in my head to keep my limbs moving in rhythm. I wanted to tell Piper this—in fact, I wished I had told her earlier, back on the beach—but it was too hard to explain while we were breathless at sea. Piper had no idea how to pace herself in the water, and she was burning up her energy with her panicky shallow breathing and awkward water treading.

Just when I started to feel the burn, Luke said, "Let's hit it, ladies!" and he started swimming parallel to the beach. Piper and I followed. I kept a close eye on her at first, swimming sidestroke with my head above water. As she swam, Piper lifted her eyes every now and then to try to stay on course, but she was chopping around all over the place; looking up only seemed to disorient her more.

Finally, I had to put my head down and swim butterfly for a bit—the sidestroke was tiring me out. Today the pacing song playing in my head was that old one, "Renegades" by the X Ambassadors; it had a perfect beat for my stroke. When I paused after a stretch, I saw that I had pulled far ahead of Piper, who was really drifting off course and out to sea. She looked up once to see me glancing back at her. I stopped and treaded in place for a minute. But Piper's strokes had grown slow; she was fatigued and beginning to look like she was swimming in place. I saw her look longingly toward the shore, and I suddenly began to wonder if she might be in trouble. *"Do not let your partner out of your sight. Do not leave your partner behind."*

I whipped around to look for Luke, but he was way far ahead of us now, swimming freestyle with his head in the water. I called out to him, but he couldn't hear me. Looking back, I could see Piper had stopped and was treading water. This was not good. It looked like she had run out of gas.

She was about thirty yards behind me, and about ten yards father out than I was.

It was time for me to go get her.

"Luke!" I called again, but he still didn't hear me. With a heavy shake of my head, I turned back and began swimming toward Piper. *"Do not let your partner out of your sight. Do not leave your partner behind."*

As I drew near, I shouted to Piper. "Are you okay?"

Piper stared at me for a second. I could see she was about to cry. Piper shook her head *No*. She was not okay.

I felt a little frisson of panic then. Could I handle this? But what was the alternative? I had to act confident.

"C'mon, then. Let's go in. You can do this."

Piper shook her head again. "I'm scared." Her mouth bunched into crying position.

"You have to get moving now, Piper. You're strong. Let's go," I encouraged.

But Piper stayed put, treading. It looked like she was anchored in place. I was going to have to get tough.

"NOW!" I yelled, and the force of my voice shocked Piper into moving.

Side by side, we began swimming for shore. I did a modified breaststroke (my weakest stroke) so I could keep my head above water and watch Piper. Piper shook raindrops out of her eyes and after a few seconds said, "Luke," so I turned to look. There was Luke, turning around and heading back toward us.

Too little, too late, I thought in annoyance. *Who cares how cute he is now?*

And then we were at the break, and a set of larger waves reached it just as we did. I grabbed Piper's arm to hold her back—we needed to time this right or we'd get crushed—but Piper flung it off. Now that the shore was so close, there was no stopping her.

"Piper!" I shouted. "Stop! We have to wait!"

But Piper was in a panic. I'm sure she figured she'd just ride a wave in and be finished with it all. But then Piper realized her mistake, and she stalled right at the worst possible place. She was between waves, and the next one was shaping up to crest behind her. It would carry her over and flip her for sure if she didn't either swim in or back out. She was caught.

"Piper!" I yelled in a panic. "Swim!"

I flung myself forward and swam hard, but I didn't reach Piper in time. I held back to intentionally miss the wave ride as Piper surged ahead. She wound up in the crest of the wave and was thrown mercilessly head over heels, while I could only watch, horrified. The ocean tumbled her into a somersault, and I was sure her head was crunching into the sand on the ocean floor as her body spun like a sock in a washing machine. She had disappeared under the surface.

I rode the next wave in and stumbled through the whitewater, searching for Piper. Then, out of nowhere, Luke surged out of the water, holding Piper under her arms and shaking foam from his eyes. *How in the world had he found her?* He steadied Piper onto her feet, sort of, and the two of them stumbled onto the sand, sitting down heavily. I followed them and collapsed in exhaustion at Piper's side.

"Luke! Girls!" Mr. Slater shouted as he reached us, a small white towel in each hand (the kind they rent out at the beach office for three dollars a day). He dropped to one knee and looked at us in concern. "Are you all right?" he asked breathlessly, as he handed us the tiny towels.

Piper nodded and I looked at him, unsure of what to say. Piper had a huge sand burn up her thigh; it was red and I'm sure it was throbbing, though Piper might not have felt it yet.

But Slater wanted a real answer. "I'm not just being polite. Are you all right? Can you speak? Do you know where you are?"

I cleared my throat. "Yes. I'm fine," I said.

He looked at Piper.

"Me too," agreed Piper. "Just a little wobbly." She managed a small smile.

"Anything hurt?" pressed Slater.

Piper shook her head. "No."

"Just that," I said, pointing to her leg.

Slater nodded. "We can take care of that up in the office. That's gonna be real sore later." Then he stood up and turned to his son. "Your hotdogging out there caused something dangerous to happen. There was no need to turn on the turbo when you were supposed to be swimming with the girls."

"But..." Luke looked at his father in disbelief. "I got back in time."

"Barely!" snapped his dad.

Piper and I looked away for a second, embarrassed to be witnessing this family fight and sorry to be the cause of it.

When I peeked back at him, Luke had set his jaw and turned away from his father to look back out at the ocean.

"It was this one—a child, untrained—who had to save her friend!" Mr. Slater seemed to be working himself up.

"All right, Dad. I get it," said Luke, still cross but trying to defuse the situation.

"You'd better, son!" Bud Slater looked at Luke piercingly for a minute, and we could all see him decide to let it go for now. Then he shook his head, deflated. "After all we've been through, with Molly..."

Luke looked pained, but then anger flared in his eyes. He jumped to his feet. "*You're* the one who said we can't let that accident get inside our heads. *You're* the one who said, 'Fear ruins lifeguards.' Right, Dad? *Right*?" he demanded, his hands on his hips.

Slater looked away, his jaw working.

What were they talking about? Was it...? Could it be...?

"Wait, um..." I didn't want to interrupt a family row, but suddenly I had to know. I stood. "Did something happen? Who are you talking about?"

Luke looked at me, his eyes blazing. "Molly Cruise. Star lifeguard. My dad's pride and joy. And now her career is ruined. All because my dad taught her to 'never walk away from danger,'" Luke scoffed.

"That's enough!" roared Slater.

Piper and I flinched, but Luke set his jaw defiantly.

"Wait, wh... Molly Cruise? What happened?" I felt a clutching in my chest. "Did she... Is she okay?"

Slater spoke very quietly, looking offshore into the distance. "She was on Easter break in Mexico, with friends. Another girl was drinking. The girl went in the water, didn't come out. The waves were big..." He shook his head, and I could see his eyes were welling.

I grabbed his arm. "What happened?"

He looked at me like he was waking from a dream. "Molly went in to save her friend and suffered a traumatic spinal injury. She has to learn how to walk again."

I couldn't breathe. "No! And the other girl?"

Slater cleared his throat. "Not a scrape. Walked away fine." He laughed mirthlessly, a sharp bark.

My eyes welled with tears. "Where is Molly now?"

"Mid-Cape," said Slater. "Saint Sebastian's Rehabilitation Center. Coach Randall and I have gone to see her every week since she got there in mid-April."

Saint Sebastian's. MC. It was all coming together. My mother's notes on the phone pad. Coach Randall and Slater talking about traffic. Coach Randall's occasional lateness to practice.

Molly!

The tears spilled over the rims of my eyes. "I can't believe it. She was my idol," I said quietly. I blotted at my eyes furiously with the tiny white towel. I could feel Piper staring at me. I knew she'd quit now, but I didn't care. Something powerful welled inside me, whether it was fear, or grief, or craziness, I do not know. All I knew was that I *had* to be a lifeguard now. I had to do it for me *and* Molly.

Slater turned back to us. "I'm sorry to be the bearer of bad news. Let's go, Luke. There are a couple more kids to go." He seemed deflated, diminished, all of a sudden. "Nice work out there, Bowers. You kept your wits about you. You're a strong swimmer. I'm impressed. And Janssens, you don't quit, do you?"

Piper shook her head, but I wasn't sure it meant what he thought. I read it as *There is no way I'm doing this crazy program*. Slater probably saw it as, *I'm not a quitter; I'll be back for more*.

"Kids, bad stuff happens. But there are rules, guidelines, and techniques. I can teach it all to you, and it will help you save people, and even save yourselves, if it comes to that. It's when emotions get in the way that you're in trouble in the ocean."

He walked away from us, back up the sand toward the pavilion, his head and shoulders hanging. He looked old.

As soon as he was out of earshot, Piper whispered, "I'm so sorry, both of you."

I waved it off. I couldn't stop thinking about Molly.

Luke shook his head, rueful and apologetic. "It was totally my fault. I just got a rhythm and kept going. I thought you were both strong ocean swimmers and this test was just a formality. I should have turned back to check. I'm sorry."

"I'm sorry your dad got mad at you because of me," said Piper quietly.

"Ha!" Luke laughed mirthlessly. "My dad only gets mad at me because of me. You'll soon see that. Speaking of which, I'd better go face the music."

He patted Piper on her back, but Piper's face didn't even light up from his touch; she was that wiped out. "I'm sorry about Molly. And I'm sorry you had to find out that way," he said.

"Is she going to be okay?" I asked urgently.

Luke nodded. "But it's going to take a lot of work and probably a year out of her life, just relearning everything." He shook his head and jogged away.

Piper peeled off her rash guard with shaking fingers. "This is going in the garbage." Then she really looked at me. "Jenna, thank you for saving my life out there today. I really almost didn't make it. I'm so sorry about Molly. Are you okay? You're super-pale..."

I shook my head. My teeth were starting to chatter.

I needed my towel and I needed to get home and get warm. I wanted so badly to call my mom and have her come get me, but she was working at the farm stand. Sunday mornings are always super busy, rain or shine, as people load up to take stuff back to their real life off the Cape. Maybe I could call her anyway. I was sure she'd come.

"I want my mom," I said.

Piper nodded and threw her arm around my shoulder as we walked up the beach. I swallowed hard. I didn't want to cry again. I'd done more crying in the past three days than I had in the past three months!

Now Ziggy and Selena were upon us, chattering a mile a minute.

"OMG! Jenna! Are you okay? And what about you Piper? What happened? I almost went in after you, I was so worried." Ziggy's tiny face was drawn and pale with concern.

I was too stunned to even laugh at the notion of Ziggy

coming in after us. Selena reached over and grabbed me in a sideways hug, which I returned.

"Thanks," I said. Selena's eyes were big with worry.

To my surprise, Piper shook it all off. "We're fine. I just got a little overwhelmed out there, and Jenna saved me. I'm sure I failed, but she passed with flying colors."

I turned swiftly to look at her. "I'm sure I failed too. That whole thing was a disaster," I said.

"*Seriously, Jenna?* You saved me out there!" exclaimed Piper. "I just can't believe we lived to tell the tale. Lifeguarding is super dangerous," said Piper. "Even if there are cute boys."

As for me, I could not stop thinking about Molly Cruise and the news Slater had told me. I was dreading Piper telling the others too. It would turn into a huge drama, and I didn't have the energy to deal with it at the moment. I needed to get home and see what my parents knew first. Luckily, Piper didn't bring it up again.

Ziggy was adamant about our test. "I'm sure you'll

both pass. Other than at the end, you guys looked great out there. I promise. Plus, you're both like, so strong and such good people. Anyone could see you'd make awesome lifeguards," Ziggy effused. Have I mentioned that Ziggy can be a little over the top sometimes?

"How did your test go, Selena?" I asked, seeing that she had just gotten out of the water.

Selena shrugged. "It was much shorter than yours. We didn't go out nearly as far and we did it really quick. I guess I passed. I mean, nothing bad happened."

I nodded.

"And what about *your* test?" Piper asked Ziggy. Ziggy shrugged. "My parents still wouldn't sign, and forging the release is plain old illegal. I came just to see what the test was like and to ask Slater if he'll let me try it next week."

"Hey!" said Piper, remembering. "Did you get to talk to Jack Lee while you waited?"

Ziggy rolled her eyes. "Well, I tried to, but he's mute. Gorgeous, but mute. And if I can't get him to talk, no one can."

"Still waters?" asked Piper hopefully.

"Maybe a shallow pond. But very, very fine-looking! We'll see," said Ziggy.

We reached the group on the porch; there was no sign of Hayden, unfortunately, and I wasn't willing to ask Selena if he'd returned while we'd been out. The kids we knew surged around us to get the details, and the kids we didn't know looked curiously at Piper and me, like we were some kind of celebrities; they'd obviously witnessed the mini-drama in the water. It took a minute to tell everyone we were fine, just freezing and in desperate need of our towels. Finally, they let us go.

I crossed the pavilion to retrieve my towel from the bench where I'd left it, but the towel was gone. Selena, Ziggy, and Piper all helped me look around at the other nearby benches and tables, underneath and everything. Then Ziggy tapped me on the shoulder and pointed across to the opposite end of the pavilion. We all turned to look.

There, poised on the rail of the pavilion as gracefully

as a mermaid, was the Frankel girl, casually wrapped in a blue towel with the name Jenna embroidered on it in yellow for all to see.

"Oh my God, of all the nerve," breathed Piper.

"Oh, Dios mío," said Selena, shaking her head.

11

Testing

Awkward!

"Um..." I said to my friends.

"Let's go get it! It's not like she can't afford her own towel!" huffed Piper.

Ziggy leaned in. "Do you want me to go say something?"

"Please don't make me go," implored Selena, looking like she'd rather die than reprimand a Frankel girl.

The Frankel girl looked over at us without seeming to see us. Then she blinked and turned back to watch the ocean, pulling the towel a little tighter around her shoulders.

I sighed heavily. All I wanted was to be warm and dry. I shook my head and walked over to where the girl was perched.

"You *go*, girlfriend!" said Piper in a sassy voice. But I wasn't angry, exactly. More surprised that someone would take a stranger's towel without even asking. Then again, I'd swam in the Frankels' pool many times without asking, and I was a stranger to them.

"Excuse me?" I said, when I reached the bathing beauty.

The girl looked up. She had a neutral look on her face, but it was a little intentionally vague or guarded, like she was used to being flagged down in public and didn't want to seem too open.

"You have my towel," I said.

"Hmm? Oh!" the girl stood up and swung the towel off her shoulders in a graceful arc, as if it were a mink cape. "You are such a doll for lending it to me," she said in a deep, honeyed voice with an English accent. "It's divinely soft and I was chilled to the bone, waiting to see if I'd be allowed to take the test. Thanks *ever* so much."

It was weird to hear such an adult voice coming from someone who looked to be about my own age. And lending? Seriously? But at least she was nice. I'd been ready to be kind of cold to this girl. Now I was at a loss.

"Uh. Yes. Right. Okay," I stammered.

The girl chatted on. "No one would ever think to buy me a towel of my very own, just for me, with my name on it like this. My mum might throw me an Hermès towel she got as a party favor somewhere, but otherwise her interior designer just buys everything to match the décor. It's so impersonal! I'm Samantha," said the girl, putting out her hand.

I reached my own hand out and Samantha's long, icy fingers clasped mine.

"And you are...?" prompted Samantha.

"Jenna. Jenna Bowers," I said, as Samantha pumped my hand professionally, like a businesswoman.

Then Samantha laughed a beautiful, deep laugh. (*Was Jenna Bowers a funny name?* I wondered.) She smacked her own forehead. "Aren't I silly asking you your name when it's right here on your towel?"

Oh.

I managed an idiotic grin. "Yes. That's right. Uh-huh." I was quite eloquent today, wasn't I?

I glanced over my shoulder to see Piper, Selena, and Ziggy standing and watching us. Was I supposed to befriend this person or just walk away?

"It's bleeding cold out here. That's certain," said the girl, rubbing the visible goose bumps on her arms. I suddenly felt guilty. After all, I was pretty much dry at this point, and I did have my anorak to put on. I looked at the towel clutched to my chest, then back at the basically naked girl. I thought of all the good times I'd had on her trampoline. Without her, of course.

"Do you want to keep using it?" I asked, spontaneously.

"Oh, you are *too* sweet. No. I'm okay now. I think I'll be

called up soon, and then I can just race back to the house. I'll be right as rain, thanks. Anyway, you'll need it now you're finished. What happened out there, darling?"

Darling?

Suddenly, Bud Slater was at our side.

He looked at Samantha in not the friendliest of ways. "We'll have time to fit you in, but you'd better hustle. If you pass this, then we'll waive the pool test and straighten you out about being on time and all, in the future. And don't forget: This isn't Hollywood. Lifeguards don't wear bikinis. Now scram down to the water. Luke's waiting for you." Mr. Slater was stern, and I was glad I wasn't on the receiving end of his orders. I wrapped myself tightly in my towel as he spoke.

"Thank you *ever* so much for fitting me in, you are *too* kind," said Samantha, and she strolled, unhurried, like a panther down the boardwalk, seemingly unbothered by Slater's unfriendly tone or comments about her outfit.

I wanted desperately to ask him what the deal was

with Hayden right then, or even some more questions about Molly. I was just summoning my courage when Slater spoke.

"Imagine a parent letting their kid out of the house dressed like that? What are people thinking?" He shook his head in disbelief.

I followed his gaze down to the ocean where Samantha and Luke were meeting and chatting. I thought of Imari and Benjamin Frankel. They probably wouldn't like the look of what Samantha was wearing right now either. But I bet Nigel probably encouraged such fashion choices, judging by the look of him in photos online.

"Maybe her parents are away in Europe and she has some babysitter who's either useless or too intimidated to tell her what to do," I said.

Slater was silent for an extra second, so I turned to look at him. He was smiling and nodding.

"Good answer, Bowers," he said finally.

I looked back at the water. "Thank you, sir," I said,

taking a page from Ziggy's book. When in doubt, go military.

Still nodding to himself, Slater walked away to lean on the railing of the pavilion and watch the final test.

Well, at least Slater knows my name, I thought, as I returned to my friends to say goodbye. Even if I don't make the crew (to my eye, no one had obviously failed today, except possibly me and Piper), I was wiped out now that all the adrenaline had worn off, and I wanted to get home and into my cozy clothes.

Ziggy and Piper scrambled to meet me halfway, asking all sorts of questions about Samantha. Selena hung back, as if embarrassed by the whole incident.

I minimized the whole thing and told them Samantha was really nice. Which she was. I glanced at Selena and could see relief wash over her face. Dissatisfied with the lack of gossip, Ziggy and Piper stood next to me, and we all found ourselves watching Samantha's test.

It was just Samantha and Luke, and from the get-go it

looked like a date. There was a lot of splashing each other, then what looked like chasing (Luke chasing Samantha), and I could feel Piper growing indignant by my side. Luke and Samantha were having a good time out there and what's more, Samantha was a truly beautiful swimmer. I felt a twinge thinking about my own swimming and leaving the team. If Piper was jealous of Samantha because of Luke, then I was jealous because of Samantha's gorgeous stroke.

Piper burst into my quiet thoughts. "Come *on!* It's like those two are in love or something!" she huffed.

Ziggy nodded. "Yeah." Selena didn't say anything.

I didn't know *what* to say. I kind of felt sorry for Samantha, but I didn't want to make Piper mad by defending her.

"Don't you think it's a little much?" Piper prompted me, as Luke and Samantha began swimming in tandem across the shoreline, like synchronized swimmers.

I glanced at Mr. Slater, who was standing now with his arms folded across his chest, watching the swimmers intently. He didn't look too pleased either, but I figured it was Luke and not Samantha who was causing the displeasure.

I sighed. "Yeah," I said finally, remembering my loyalties. "I think it's...outrageous." But I didn't say it with quite enough emphasis, and Piper turned to look at me to see if I was being sarcastic. I kept my face expressionless. After what happened in the ocean, my affection for Luke had dwindled, but if Piper's hadn't, I didn't want to hurt her feelings.

"It's like Luke Slater is her boyfriend!" protested Piper.

"Well, he *is* a lot older than you, Pipe," I said finally.

I glanced at her, and she nodded a little and sighed. We'd be dissecting this information for weeks to come.

Samantha had finished her test. She and Luke came out of the water and high-fived each other, with Samantha looking more like a model than ever with her wet hair shining and her belly chain glinting, even on this steel-gray day. Everyone who was still here was staring, and she seemed to enjoy it. She strutted up the boardwalk to the pavilion, Luke in tow. It was really too much for Piper to bear.

"Gross," she said in disgust. "And my leg is now killing me. I'm going into the office to see what they have to put on it." She turned away.

"I'll come with you," said Selena, who looked like she was dying to get away.

When Samantha reached Mr. Slater, he called out, "*Very nice, Ms. Frankel. Very nice. I think you've just snagged the last spot on the Junior Lifeguard crew for this season!*"

Whaaaaat? I felt a surge of anger. The last spot? But there weren't any spots left! I was trying out as an alternate as it was! And why would Slater be telling Samantha that now? The list wouldn't be posted until Tuesday, he'd said.

My blood started to boil. Slater hadn't been as complimentary to me after my test, and I was nearly as good a swimmer as Samantha Frankel. (Logic would point out that it was because I'd nearly drowned trying to save my friend, but that was beside the point.) Maybe Slater was whipped up by having such a glamorous swimmer teed up for his program. He had learned Samantha's name pretty quickly, that was for sure.

Hmm. Maybe Samantha Frankel wasn't going to be my new friend after all.

Just then, Jack Lee strode across the pavilion and handed a towel to Samantha. She grinned and tossed her hair as she took the towel from him, mopping her eyes and chatting away. As Ziggy and I turned to watch, Jack started chatting back to her, and they moved off to the side, engrossed in conversation.

"I thought you said he was mute," said Piper, appearing back at our side with her leg covered in some kind of ointment.

Ziggy shrugged. "He was." She bit her lip thoughtfully, her head cocked to the side.

His scolding finished, Luke rejoined the chatty twosome and offered Samantha his hoodie sweatshirt. Piper's face darkened.

"Let's go," she said. "Zigs, you need a ride?"

"Sure. Can I throw my bike in the back?"

"Selena? You walking?" asked Piper.

Selena, who had been silent this whole time, finally spoke. "Yeah. Thanks. Listen guys... This is just really awkward. My mom is worried about the Frankels. She thinks Nigel, their babysitter or whatever, is an unreliable nightmare. So, she's taken it upon herself to organize the girls, and she's the one who signed the form for Samantha so she could come down here today. I feel bad that she's causing all these bad feelings. It's so embarrassing. But I'm like...the help, so it's really awkward?"

Poor Selena. What a tough spot to be in, I thought. "It's okay, Leeny," I said. "We don't hold you responsible. She was really nice to me, remember? And those boys can't help themselves. She's like...an international celebrity. And she's gorgeous! Who could resist?"

"Thanks, Jen," said Selena. We were both kind of waiting for Ziggy and Piper to say it wasn't Selena's fault, but they were silent, watching Samantha, Luke, and Jack Lee laugh their heads off together across the pavilion.

"It will all settle down. Don't worry," I said, silently hoping I was right.

We gathered our gear and made for the parking lot. I glanced back as we left, just in time to see Samantha waving at me. Or maybe she was waving at Selena? But Selena either hadn't seen the wave or was ignoring Samantha.

I felt I had to wave back. But in a totally dorky move, I dropped my towel as I went to wave at her, making me look overly enthusiastic.

When I came up from picking up my towel, I found Piper giving me an odd look.

"What?" I asked innocently. But Piper didn't reply.

In the parking lot, Piper's grandma Bett hopped out of the truck to help us with our gear. She pulled the hood of her yellow fisherman's rain slicker up over her short silver hair. Under the slicker, she wore her usual uniform of riding jodhpurs, beat up riding boots, and a polo shirt. Today she'd added a wool sweater as a concession to the weather.

"How was it?" Bett asked in a chipper voice. "Great?"

"It was okay," Piper shrugged.

"Well, it will certainly be fun for you girls to do that program together this summer," said Bett, brightly.

Ziggy was about to interject but Piper spoke up first.

"I...I actually failed, Bett," said Piper quietly. I could see she was holding back tears all of a sudden.

"You don't know that, Piper. Slater loves you," I protested. "If anyone failed, it was me, for letting you almost drown," I added.

"Oh, Jenna. Don't be so hard on yourself!" said Selena.

Piper's grandmother moved to Piper's side and began speaking in low, comforting tones, like she was soothing a wild stallion. She was tough on the outside, old Bett, but inside she was a really kind person.

Suddenly Ziggy said, "OMG."

Selena and I followed her gaze, and there was Ziggy's father, getting out of his Prius at the edge of the lot.

"Dad!" called Ziggy, trotting across the parking lot. "Oh my gosh! I can't believe you came!"

Her father looked around in confusion. "Ziggy?" he said. "What are you doing here?"

Ziggy stopped and stood stock-still. "Wait. Aren't you here for my Junior Lifeguard test?"

Her father's eyebrows drew together in confusion. "No. I'm here to check on the plovers in the rain."

Ziggy deflated like a tired party balloon. "Oh," she said in a small voice.

"I thought you weren't doing that," said her father. "I thought that was settled."

Ziggy was indignant now, and we could see she had just decided to go for it.

"Well, it's not! I took the swim test at the rec center yesterday, and I passed! Slater really likes me. He said he likes my smile. And he invited me to take the test here today only..." She paused.

"Only what?" said her dad, pulling his windbreaker sharply closed and zipping it roughly against the wet breeze.

"Only I needed an adult to sign the release form in order to be allowed to do it."

Ziggy's dad crossed his arms and puffed his lips out. "So, you came anyway, even though you knew you couldn't take the test?"

Ziggy nodded morosely. "I thought maybe I could ask him if I could take the test another time."

"So, *did* you ask him?"

"Not yet. I was chicken."

Her dad was quiet. He looked at her, and then he looked around the parking lot and the beach. Finally, after what seemed like an endless wait, he said, "Ziggy, honey?"

"Yes?"

"Let's go take that test. If you pass, then we'll decide what's next. What do you say?"

"Really?" Ziggy looked like she could hardly believe it! "Are you serious?"

"Yup. Let's go." They walked quickly across the parking lot, back to the pavilion, and her dad peppered her with questions as they moved away from us. "Have you eaten any protein? Did you stretch? Have you done some relaxing breathing?"

"Oh, Dad!" protested Ziggy.

Selena and I laughed as they walked away. I shook my head. "That Ziggy! She always comes out on top!" said Selena.

"Call me later," I replied, giving her a quick hug.

She hugged me back, hard. "Thanks for being a good friend, Jenna."

"You too," I said, giving her one last squeeze.

I threw my bike into Bett's truck and hopped in. Piper and Bett climbed in right after me, and although I could see Piper had been crying, she was all right now.

"Ready? Where to, girls?" said Bett.

We told her my house, and she did a U-turn and drove us away from that freezing beach.

Piper leaned over and whispered. "She said I could go back to the barn if I fail."

I nodded and looked out the window as we passed Selena trudging alone down Ocean Road.

"Great," I said unenthusiastically. "That's great."

12

Lessons

Monday was a blur of school, studying for the exams that would start Wednesday, and me trying to distract myself from wondering if I'd passed the Junior Lifeguard test. There was only a week of school left, and it was weird not to know what my summer held for me—everything was up in the air until I heard the result.

Slater had told us he'd post the list at the rec center on Tuesday, so after school that day, I rode my bike there directly. Fast.

Slater's pickup truck was in the parking lot, and so was Coach Randall's Acura. That was a good sign. There was another bike in the rack but that was all. I lingered for a minute, not wanting to seem too eager and also, a tiny bit, wanting to prolong the possibility that I might have made it, just in case I hadn't. I'd ridden so quickly that I was sweating lightly, and I had beaten any other kid who might have left the school at the same time as I had. I didn't think anyone wanted this as badly as I did. Not just for my own sake but now for Molly's too.

After my parents got home on Sunday, Piper and I had told them everything that had happened during our test, and they said we were crazy to think for a minute that we hadn't passed. We'd stuck together, followed directions, and showed great teamwork and common sense. But in the same conversation, we discussed Molly Cruise, and they told us everything they knew about what had happened to her and what her prognosis was. Piper was more freaked out by the story than I was. For me, it was a fluke. A freak accident. And it made Molly more of a hero than ever, as far as I was concerned. Unlike Piper, it just fanned the fire inside me.

My parents were less positive about the story and wondered if there was a way to make sure we wouldn't have to swim in the ocean on red flag days at the beach. (At the Westham beaches, green flag meant "calm," yellow flag meant "caution," and red flag meant "dangerous, do not go into the water." The very words gave me a chill.) But I thought it was a terrible idea; I didn't want to be babied. Slater calling me "Poolie" still rang in my ears. I was adamant that if I were lucky enough to have made it, I would participate to the fullest. I certainly wouldn't want Slater to think my mommy and daddy were protecting me. And anyway, Slater would be more vigilant than ever this year. I *wanted* to learn how to handle myself in tough conditions. I *wanted* to be the person who jumped in even when everyone else was scared to. I *wanted* to be...just like Molly. Except for the injured part. That I did *not* want.

I leaned against the rec center bike rack and took a few deep breaths to steel myself. Then, with sweaty palms, I entered the building. I imagined the list would be posted on the bulletin board where I'd first seen Luke hanging the tryout poster. But there was nothing up that I hadn't seen yet. I peeked my head into Coach Randall's office, and she was there behind her desk, doing some paperwork.

I rapped lightly on her door. "Coach?" I said.

"Jenna! How lovely to see you! Come on in!" she cried.

It felt good to be warmly received.

I sat on her guest chair, we chatted briefly, and then I turned to the topic that was at the back of my mind all the time now. "I can't believe what I heard about Molly Cruise," I said, explaining about her being our sitter, how much I'd always looked up to her, and how she was the reason I'd wanted to do Junior Lifeguards to begin with.

Coach Randall's smile faded. "It has been a heck of a thing for her and her family," she said, shaking her head. "But those Cruises are strong, and they're a tight family, with a supportive church community helping them, and she's going to be okay, thank goodness. She's lucky to be alive."

"Mr. Slater said it's going to be a long road to recovery for her," I said.

Coach Randall nodded. "She's a fighter, though. She'll come through." Then she tipped her head and looked at me. "Hey! I just had an idea. Would you like to come with me and Bud Slater to see Molly this weekend?"

My eyebrows flew up in the air. "Really? Do you think that would be okay? I mean, I don't want to crash your outing or, like, embarrass Molly. It would be so cool to see her, though!"

Coach Randall smiled and nodded. "I'll put in a call to Mrs. Cruise to see if it's okay, and then I'll call and check with your mom too. If it all works out, then I'll text you what time to meet us here, okay?"

"Great. Thank you so much!"

"And you're coming to practice on Friday night?" Friday was always our hardest swim team practice of the week.

"Wouldn't miss it!" I said, with a laugh, because now I'd be missing a lot of practices.

"I'm so glad."

I took a deep breath. "So...do you know when Mr. Slater is going to post the list?" I asked. The butterflies in my stomach took flight as I thought of it again.

"I don't know. He *is* here somewhere, though. I saw him...maybe... I think he might be giving a lesson in the pool, actually. Why don't you pop your head in and check? If he's not busy, you can ask him or otherwise just wait till the lesson is over."

"Cool. Thanks, Coach. And thanks so much about the visit with Molly."

"It's my pleasure. Good luck with the lifeguarding!" she said, cheerily.

I left her office and tried to decide if that meant she knew whether or not I'd made it. Like, was she saying, "Good luck... I hope you *make* the lifeguarding program," or "Good luck doing it because I *know* you made it."?

I decided to go through the ladies' locker room and look through the window in the door to see if I could see Slater inside the pool room. That way, I wouldn't have to enter the room and possibly interrupt him; I was scared to annoy him, especially at this point.

The locker room was dead quiet and empty, and I thought of all the time I'd spent in this place over the years: both happy and stressful, but sometimes even peaceful. I love to swim, and I love the water and thinking about possibly becoming a lifeguard one day excited me so much. My butterflies were flapping their wings, and my palms were sweating as my sneakers squeaked across the tile floor.

At the door to the pool room, I reached over and flicked off the locker room lights, so I could see in better and also so no one would see me if they looked my way. All I needed was Slater to think I was stalking him.

I took a deep breath and peered through the window. A glass wall on one side and overhead pendants throughout the room brightly illuminated the pool room. Sure enough, there was Bud Slater in the shallow end of the pool in a bathing suit. He was giving a lesson to someone who was doing a facedown dead man's float, so a real beginner. Slater wasn't supporting the person, but he hovered nearby, his hands in the air on the alert to snatch the person if they faltered. He wasn't saying anything that I could hear. As I looked, I realized the person was male and quite big. Maybe he was even an adult. It wouldn't surprise me if Slater gave free lessons to the new immigrants who came to town. I knew that despite his tough persona, he was a charitable guy.

I sighed. Now I'd have to wait until this lesson was over before I'd hear anything. I looked at my watch; if it were a half-hour lesson, it would be over in ten minutes, and then he'd need time to dry off and post the list. Half an hour. I decided I'd go sit outside on a bench and do what little homework I had.

I flicked the lights back on and took one last glimpse through the window, just as the swimmer sputtered and stood. We locked eyes. It was Hayden Jones.

Quickly, I turned on my heel and fled out the door of the locker room, my shoes banging on the tiles as I ran. My face was burning with shame at my nosiness, and I wished nothing more than that I could unsee what I had just seen.

Hayden Jones couldn't swim. He was fourteen years old and planning to train as a lifeguard for the summer, a preppy boarding school kid, obviously an athlete, and he could not swim.

I ran though the rec center lobby and smashed open the door and found myself out on the sidewalk, shaking and mortified. As luck would have it, all the kids had started arriving from school to check the list. There were probably twelve kids walking toward the door. I didn't want anyone to see what I had just seen. I wanted to preserve Hayden's dignity.

I stretched my arms out to my sides to bar entry to the rec center.

"The list is not ready, people! Slater said to wait out

here until four fifteen, and he will post it and call us all in!" I announced, mentally crossing my fingers at the fib.

People stopped. They listened. And they believed me. They began settling themselves down on the lawn and benches to wait. I flopped onto a bench and took a deep breath to settle my nerves, and just then, Piper, Selena, and Ziggy appeared and joined me.

"No news?" asked Selena, settling gracefully down next to me and tucking her legs to the side like a lady.

I shook my head and bit my tongue. I was desperate to report what I'd just seen, to let my friends calm my nerves and soothe my embarrassment and explain it all away, but I knew I couldn't. It would have been selfish. This was not about me, but about Hayden. I just wondered how a kid from a private school background, who lived in Florida, for goodness' sake, had gotten this far without ever learning to swim! And more importantly, how did he think he could be a lifeguard if he couldn't swim?

Piper slung her arm around my neck. "Don't look so nervous, missy. I'm sure you made it."

"If anyone made it, you did," agreed Ziggy, loyally. She had been given her ocean test by Bud Slater himself after we'd left the other day. He'd told her dad she had a great attitude, and her dad had softened toward him and promised Ziggy that if she made Junior Lifeguards, he'd talk her mom into letting her do it.

"Thanks, Zigs."

Selena sighed and pouted a little. "My dad said if I didn't make it, I have to do summer school for sure. So now I'm hoping I *did* make it even though I don't really want to do it!"

"*I* want to do it!" said Ziggy. "Jack Lee said hi to me at the library yesterday when I was checking my email. And I'm sure *he'll* make it!"

"No way, Zigs! Good for you!" I was glad for her.

She smiled and wiggled a little in happiness. "Hey, is he here?" she started looking for him but to no avail.

Selena leaned in and whispered. "I hope Samantha doesn't make it. I know that's really mean of me to say, but it would be so awkward to have to hang with her all summer."

I nodded. "I hear you. But I bet she made it. Slater *said* she'd made it. Look, she seems nice..." I whispered back. I didn't want Piper to hear me and think I was being disloyal.

Selena nodded her head kind of wishy-washy. "Yeah... I don't know. Her life is so different. And she could pick up and leave at a moment's notice anyway. There's no point in investing in a friendship." Selena rolled her eyes. "But Hugo sure thinks she's nice."

"Really?! Saint Hugo?" I laughed. Selena's brother is gorgeous, but he's a hard worker and also does all this volunteer work and stuff all the time; adults love him and sometimes we all find it really annoying. "When would he even have the time to *notice* she's nice? Did she help him polish his halo or something?"

Selena laughed. "He was helping my dad fix some

brickwork around the pool and Samantha came out and they started chatting and I guess they really hit it off. She's in Model UN like him and really into it, so...whatever. It's not like she'd date him, anyway. He's her caretaker's son." Selena shrugged.

"So?" I said.

"Jenna. Seriously? Grow up," scoffed Selena.

"Anyone would be a fool not to date Hugo," said Piper, dreamily. We all laughed. She'd always had a crush on him, but it was almost like a formality at this point. Nothing would ever happen there and anyway; Piper was so liberal with her crushes. She once crushed on the school bus driver, two eighth graders, and the Starbucks guy all in twenty minutes.

I glanced at my watch. Only five minutes had passed. Not enough time for Slater to have posted the list. I sighed and stretched. My nerves had settled down, and now my curiosity was piqued. I wondered what Hayden's backstory was. I wanted to learn more.

Just then, the door to the rec center opened and everyone's head whipped up to look. But it wasn't Slater.

It was Hayden.

My breath caught and my cheeks began to redden. He looked around and spotted me and then headed right for me with a serious look on his face.

"Jenna?" he said.

"Hey...H-Hayden," I stammered awkwardly. My friends watched in curiosity.

"Can you talk for a minute? In private?" I stood nervously. "Sure...."

He set off for the far end of the parking lot, and I followed him, not looking back to see my friend's reactions. My mind was spinning. Obviously, he knew I'd seen him, so pretending I hadn't was out of the question. It was too late for that.

We rounded the corner of the building until we were out of sight of the other kids, and when he stopped, I stopped. He turned around and looked so distraught, I thought he might cry.

"Hayden..." instinctively I reached my arms out and he grabbed me into a hug and held on. I could feel him taking deep breaths, but I didn't think he was full-on crying. I have three brothers and I know boys can cry just as much as girls; they just get conditioned *not* to over time. So, I wasn't horrified at the idea of him crying in my arms, but I just felt bad. The poor guy. I patted his back and gave it a reassuring rub, just like my mom always does. Pat, pat, pat, rub, rub, rub. For the moment, I wasn't even thinking about what a crush I had on him. I mostly just felt sad for him.

Though, he was a good hugger...and tall...and cozy. Hmmm.

Finally, he took a last deep breath and pulled away. "Thanks. Sorry," he said, blushing deeply.

"Hayden...what's up?" I asked, my skin cooling as the heat of him evaporated.

He laughed a little, but his eyes were glassy and red-rimmed now. "I was supposed to tell you my life story over an ice-cream cone, remember?"

I smiled. "I'll take an IOU."

He shook his head and took a deep breath, looking off to the far edge of the playing field next to the rec center. "In no particular order: My dad split a long time ago. He has a new family, and I don't fit into that scene at all; neither of us wants me there. My mom is in rehab in Florida; she started taking sleeping pills when my dad left, and it just grew into something she couldn't control anymore. I got 'asked to leave' my boarding school because I got so depressed, I cut all my classes and said a bad word to a teacher, and so I was sent home in May. But there is no 'home' right now so...long story... The Slaters took me in for the summer. Or maybe... well...indefinitely." He sighed and looked back at me quickly and then away again, the jaws in his muscle working, and his dark eyes a little watery.

My jaw had dropped without me even realizing it. I shut my mouth. "Hayden! I'm so sorry! That's all major stuff!"

"And I guess you know now that I can't swim. I had to

hide in the bathroom during the testing. Somehow, I never learned, so Bud's teaching me in his free time. He's been really good to me."

"But how will you do lifeguards?" I asked. "I mean, if you make it."

Hayden barked out a short, mirthless laugh. "Oh, I'll make it, even if it's just for dryland training. Bud wants me to be by his side this summer so he can keep an eye on me and instill some parenting lessons I apparently never got..."

I thought back to the handshake conversation at the ocean test on Sunday and nodded my head. "Gotcha. Are you working too?"

Hayden nodded. "Coach Randall hired me to do cleaning at the rec center when I'm not doing Junior Lifeguards. Their usual guy had to go to summer school."

"Wow." I shook my head in disbelief.

"I know," he said with a small smile. "Sorry to dump this all on you. I just... I don't have any friends here yet... and I'm pretty used to having lots of friends around..."

I smiled. "I can tell. You have that 'life of the party' way about you."

Hayden laughed. "Thanks. I think. Anyway, I know you saw me in there...in the pool. And I'd really appreciate it if...I mean, I might never make any friends if people think I'm super dorky and can't even swim." He plunged his hands into the pockets of his chino shorts and looked up at the sky and then down at his feet. His dark, wavy hair was shiny in the late afternoon sun. He squinted at me.

I held my hand up in the air. "First of all, you do have a friend here and it is me. And I will also share my other friends with you. And second of all, your secret—actually, all of them is safe with me. I mean, if you do Junior Lifeguards, it will probably have to come out sooner or later that you're not much of a swimmer, but that's up to you."

Hayden sighed in huge relief. "Thank you, Jenna. That is so great of you. I'm just...sort of out of my element here, you know?"

I tipped my head and studied him. "You won't be for

long," I said (especially with looks like that, I added in my head).

Hayden squinted at me. "Slater was right about you."

"Slater? That's not good! He can't stand me!" I laughed.

Hayden's eyes widened. "Are you kidding? He thinks you're the greatest!" He started ticking things off on his fingers. "Tough, hard-working, a leader..."

Now I was totally flummoxed. "What? You must have the wrong person."

"Uh-uh! It's you. The granddaughter of some old rival of his or something?"

I smacked my forehead. "OMG. He mentioned that?"

So, Slater did know who I was!

Hayden nodded. "Yup. He told me all the stories about his own troubles growing up. I think it's why he wants to help me. His dad was kind of a deadbeat too, from what I hear."

I nodded. "I heard that too."

"Anyway, he told me I should stick with you. That you're a winner."

"Seriously?" Hayden nodded.

"He also said you're a little cocky..." teased Hayden.

I whacked him on the arm and laughed. "Am not!"

Just then, Piper's head popped out from around the corner of the rec center.

"Jenna!" she yelled. "Come on! Slater's posting the list!"

I waved my thanks, and she nodded and disappeared.

Hayden and I looked at each other.

"You're in good hands. You're going to be okay," I said.

Hayden nodded and I was worried he might cry again, but he didn't. He seemed much better now and actually smiled. "Thanks. It might be an okay summer, after all."

"It will be a *great* summer. If we make Junior Lifeguards, that is. Come on! Let's find out!" I said, and I grabbed his hand and pulled him in a fast walk back to the rec center, only letting go when we got to the door.

All I could think about was how to get him to hug me again, and maybe not in a sad way next time.

Lifeguards

Kids were streaming in the doors as we arrived, and I sud- denly held back, not wanting to know.

Hayden turned and looked at me in confusion. "What? Don't you want to go in?"

I shook my head. The butterflies were hurricane-force in my stomach now, and I couldn't face the news.

"Jenna! Come on! You made it. For sure!"

I took a deep breath and steeled myself. "Okay. Okay."

Then I closed my eyes and let Hayden pull *me* by the hand inside and to the front of the line. "Open," he said.

I opened my eyes and blinked at the bulletin board. It took a second to focus. But there was a sheet of white paper with a list of about twenty names on it. I blinked again.

There, at the very top of the list, it said my name.

Jenna Bowers, Team Captain

"Whaaaaat?" I screamed with joy and threw my arms around Hayden's neck.

I couldn't believe it. And Team Captain on top of it? Unreal!

I let go of Hayden and looked for my friends. Piper, Selena, and Ziggy piled on me, shrieking and jumping up and down.

"We made it! We all made it!" squealed Ziggy.

"We are going to have the best summer ever!" I cried in reply.

Pulling away to look at them, I spied a figure off to the side. It was Bud Slater.

I extricated myself from the pile of friends and went to thank him. I put out my hand to shake his.

"Thank you, sir," I said, all business.

He nodded and looked at me appraisingly. "You're going to do great things, Bowers. Don't get overconfident because I have a lot to teach you. But I know you can handle it. We start Monday afternoon."

"Thank you, sir," I said again. "It's going to be fun."

His blue eyes twinkled a little bit, but he said in a stern voice, "It's going to be hard work, Bowers."

"Yes, sir," I agreed, nodding sharply. "Very hard. See you this weekend." I was starting to figure this guy out.

I turned back to find my friends. I had resisted pointing out to Slater that none of them had failed so a spot could open up for me, the "alternate." Somehow, I'd always known that my friends were right—that wasn't a real part of the equation.

We were all sitting around my kitchen table an hour later, eating quesadillas Selena had made and chatting about the summer before we'd all go our own ways to study for finals. Now that we knew what we'd be doing this summer, we could fill in the cracks in our schedules with work and maybe even plan some fun outings, like our annual trip to the water park an hour away or maybe an outdoor concert or drive-in movie. Give or take a boy or two, of course. (Jack Lee had made the list too, much to Ziggy's cautious delight.) I'd invited Hayden to join us for a snack back at my house, but he said he had stuff to do, and I was glad in the end that it was just my besties and me.

Ziggy sighed happily as she licked a dab of cheese from her finger. "You are such a great cook, Selena."

Selena shrugged. "I have to cook at home a lot when my mom is cooking for the Frankels or out catering. I kind of like it; at least when I have an appreciative audience. My brother is kind of a drag to cook for since he became gluten-free."

Suddenly, Ziggy had a funny look on her face.

"Zigs?" I asked. "Something the matter? Do you want to go gluten-free?"

"What? Oh. Selena talking about catering made something weird pop into my head. Just..." she waved her hand like she was waving the thought away from her mind.

"What is it?" I asked.

Ziggy's eyebrows went together again, and she lifted her hair and gathered it into a bun, which is what she does when she's gathering her thoughts. "Well...when I did my swim test with Bud Slater out in the water, he mentioned knowing my family when he was growing up out here. And something about the glamorous catered parties my grandparents were famous for?"

I shifted uncomfortably in my seat. "Oh?" I said neutrally, not wanting to make eye contact with Selena or Piper. We'd agreed in private not to mention the Bloom house on Fairview Lane to Ziggy. It was too awkward.

"Yeah. But it was just weird because...first of all, my grandparents died a long time ago and...I don't know anything of them ever being out here for anything."

"Huh," I said selecting another quesadilla from the platter even though I didn't really want it.

Ziggy shook her head hard. "He must've gotten me confused with someone else, I guess. I just hope it wasn't a case of mistaken identity that landed me on the Junior Lifeguard squad."

"Hmmm," I cleared my throat. "Well, Junior Lifeguards will be what you make of it!" I said brightly, deliberately avoiding the real topic. Ziggy gave me an odd look, but I made my face a mask of innocence.

"And Jack Lee will be there!" singsonged Piper, blessedly changing the subject.

"True!" laughed Ziggy. "That will be awesome!"

"What's awesome is that I don't have to go to summer school!" said Selena. "Even if I do have to get tutored and take stupid swim lessons."

"What's also awesome is Bett said I can still work at the barn one day a week," added Piper.

"What's awesome is we'll all be real lifeguards together one day!" I said.

"Cheers to that!" cried Piper, and we all clinked our Snapple bottles together.

Saturday afternoon came quickly, almost too quickly. I'd finished the week and the school year in a blaze of happiness. I was going to get good grades on my exams and report card; I worked really hard at swim team practice on Friday night (I even earned a compliment from Coach Randall, which wasn't easy); Hayden and I had gone for pizza in town on Friday after practice (as my mom said when I asked if I could go: it wasn't a date but more like a "friendly plan"); the Ziggy grandparent thing did not come up again; Selena was starting to stress a teeny tiny bit less about Samantha

Frankel being around (Samantha had joined them for dinner at Hugo's invitation and had gone crazy for Selena's miso cod, comparing it favorably to the one at Nobu in London); and my mom and Mrs. Cruise had agreed I could go visit Molly with Coach Randall and Bud Slater.

And now it was time to go, and I was feeling nervous. I'd admired Molly for so long and the news of her accident had been so devastating and now I wasn't sure what I'd say when I saw her. My mom and I had gone to pick out a little gift for her in town, and at least I was psyched about that. At this sweet little gift shop called Victoria's Mother, we'd found a red enamel cross on a silver chain; it was just like a lifeguard cross. It was so perfect, but I hesitated.

"Mom, do you think this might make Molly sad?" I asked. "Like, she might not be a lifeguard again."

My mom sighed. "I think it's lovely. Once a lifeguard, always a lifeguard, right?"

"I guess," I nodded.

"Plus, it will inspire her, I'm sure, to keep working on

her walking," said my mom. So, we got it, and the lady wrapped it in a tiny box with a pretty bow and we left.

Now it was in my backpack as I pedaled to the rec center.

Outside, I stowed and locked my bike and went in to find the coaches.

I knocked lightly on Coach Randall's door.

They were inside.

Slater looked at his watch. "Early as usual, Bowers."

"Sorry, sir," I said.

"I like it. In my book, five minutes early is on time, and on time is late." He stood and stretched.

I had to laugh. "That's what my dad always says!"

"Great minds think alike. Let's go. No time like the present."

I shifted my backpack uneasily from one shoulder to the other, and Slater glanced at me.

"Don't be nervous, kiddo. You're with us, and it will all be fine."

I trusted him.

In the car, we chatted some about our families. I learned that the Slaters had four kids, with Luke being the youngest. Mr. Slater implied that Luke had some learning difficulties, including dyslexia and attention-deficit/hyperactivity disorder, and school was sometimes challenging for him. No wonder he'd had a hard time with our paperwork in the office that day.

Coach Randall said her sister had dyslexia, and then she went to Stanford, so Slater shouldn't worry. "It's not the dyslexia that worries me," he said. "It's that the only thing he feels good about is his way with the ladies."

I started to feel like I was eavesdropping after a bit, so I put my earbuds in and napped. Next thing I knew, we had stopped, and Coach Randall was patting my shoulder.

"Was the practice that hard last night?" she laughed.

I unfolded myself from the back seat and looked around. We were parked next to a grassy lawn that surrounded a one-story building that looked like a seaside resort—a very well-cared-for pale-gray clapboard building with bright white trim and neat landscaping.

"Pretty," I said, and Coach Randall nodded and bit her lip.

I followed them inside, with Slater leading the way, and my butterflies lifted off and began flapping in my stomach. Why had I thought it was a good idea to come see Molly? Why did I want to do this again? As if reading my mind, Slater dropped back and looked me in the eye. "You are going to be fine. Remember, it's not about us, it's about her. She's bored as heck and thrilled for visitors. Don't be nervous. She'll just be happy you're here. And she looks just the same as usual."

I took a deep breath and nodded.

We rounded a corner and entered a bright sun porch with screened windows, white wicker furniture, and discreet handrails and walkers placed around the room. There were a few clusters of people chatting and at the far wall, I spied Molly's corn-silk yellow hair. She was sitting with her mom.

My heart leapt in happiness when I saw her. She looked the exact same! A huge grin bloomed on my face, and I hustled my step to greet her.

As I drew closer, I saw that she had complicated braces on her legs with screws and rods running the length of them, but I willed my eyes up and to her face. As she saw us, a big smile lit up her face and she waved. Her mom turned and smiled, and I knew it was all going to be okay.

I came in close and felt a little shy, but I reached out for a hug and Molly grasped me tightly. "You look awesome, Jenna! So grown up! I am so happy you came to visit!" She pulled away and held me at arm's length and smiled. "We all knew you'd be a beauty!"

I laughed, embarrassed. "Please. *You* look amazing! I'm so psyched to see you. Hi, Mrs. Cruise," I said, offering my hand for a shake. She hopped up and hugged me too, even though I didn't really know her.

"You're great to come!" she said. "Molly's tired of looking at me!"

"Never!" joked Molly. She greeted Slater and Coach Randall, and we all settled in for a chat. Coach Randall had made her famous caramel brownies, so we all ate some and then the grown-ups went to get us waters and themselves some coffee and left us girls alone to chat.

I felt the butterflies starting again at being alone with Molly. It might have been a little awkward without the grown-ups as buffers, but Molly jumped right in.

"My mom hates to hear me talk about the accident," she began, "And I'm sure you're curious—especially since I hear you're starting Junior Lifeguards. Congratulations! I'll talk fast before she gets back."

My mouth went dry and I gulped nervously. "Okay."

"I'm sure you heard that my best friend from college was drunk and almost drowned and when I tried to save her, I got hurt and she was fine?"

I nodded.

"That's not exactly how it went. Paige *is* my best friend from college, and she's the nicest person on earth. Literally. I mean, I have seen her actually give people the clothes off her back. And she has been an amazing friend to me, like when I broke up with my boyfriend, she just stayed by my side like glue and lots of other tough times. Just awesome. So that day, we met some guys and they were fun, but they must've put something in Paige's fruit drink because Paige became really out of it, and we don't even drink alcohol, even though we're of legal age now. So, we ditched those awful guys, and my other friends and I were sticking by Paige and waiting for the effects to wear off. Then I went to the bathroom, and when I came back, Paige had disappeared without the others noticing. We looked and looked for her, and then we realized one of the guys had come back and taken her out into the ocean, and the waves were *huge*. I mean, I am a really strong swimmer and I have lots of ocean experience, but I would not have chosen to go in that day, you know?"

I nodded again; my eyes wide.

"And I could see her, so I stood at the edge of the water and tried to wave her back in. The guy caught a wave to come in, but Paige just disappeared. So, what could I do? I went in and somewhere along the line, she came out in one piece and I didn't."

Molly reached over and grabbed my hand. "But Jenna, I would do the exact same thing again, you know? I would *never* stand by and watch my best friend drown without trying to save her. I took an oath when I became a life-guard. Some people don't take it seriously, but I did. I have a skill I am obligated to share, to help people. It's like being a doctor. And I'll do it again. I'll be back at it. I can guaran-tee you." She gestured down at her legs. She sat back in her chair, a look of relief on her face, as if she were glad to have unburdened herself of the story.

"I just want people to know that. I'm not bitter or regretful. I'm proud of what I did."

"So am I," I said quietly. I reached down and unzipped

my backpack and pulled out the gift box. "Here. I brought you this. You don't have to wear it, but I just…"

"Wow! Thank you, Jenna. That is so sweet. You didn't need to do that." Molly gently undid the ribbon and opened the box. She withdrew the little suede pouch and shook the chain into the palm of her hand.

"Oh!" She looked up at me and I could see the tears spring to her eyes. "Oh, Jenna! I love it! This is so…" She put her hand over her mouth and the tears rolled down. Then she dashed her eyes with her sleeve and said, "Will you help me put it on? I stink at these little clasps."

"Sure!" I said, happy to have a job. I jumped up and put the necklace on her, and she fiddled the red cross into position.

"How do I look?" she asked with a smile, blotting the tears from her cheeks.

"Awesome," I said.

We grinned at each other for a few seconds and then we could hear the adults returning from down the hall.

"I always knew you'd be a lifeguard, Jenna. You've always been an incredible swimmer and very mature and confident for your age. The other kids will listen to you." She dropped her voice to a whisper as the adults drew near. "Don't be afraid of Bud. He likes to be intimidating, but he's an excellent teacher and he's kind of a heart-whisperer, if you know what I mean? Like Yoda or Mr. Miyagi from *The Karate Kid*."

I giggled. "Yoda? Does he know you think that?"

Molly laughed and gave me a swat. "No! And don't tell him I told you!"

The adults were upon us. "Well look at these two, thick as thieves," said Slater with a smile.

Molly and I looked at him, and then we both dissolved into giggles.

"Uh-oh, telling tales, are we?" said Slater, but he didn't seem to mind.

"Molly, I love your necklace! Is that new?" said Coach Randall.

Molly put her hand to her neck. "Yes, Jenna just gave it to me. It's going to be good luck as I train my way back onto the squad."

"Oh, that is so kind," said her mom. "How pretty." But her eyes looked sad as she said it. She probably never wanted Molly to go near the ocean again.

Everyone chatted for about fifteen more minutes about Westham gossip, and then Slater stood. "I'm sorry but I have to get back because Carol's got us hosting the boys' varsity lacrosse team dinner tonight."

"Fun!" said Mrs. Cruise.

As the adults wrapped up their chat, Molly said, "Jenna, come with me to my room. I have something for you."

She reached for a pair of crutches that were tucked at her side and began to hoist herself out of the seat.

"Can I help you?" I asked, noticing that no one else was offering.

"Molly likes to do everything on her own, dear," said Mrs. Cruise, spying my helplessness. "Don't worry.

Sometimes she falls but that just fires her up even more."
She shook her head proudly.

Molly put her hands in the cuffs of the crutches and
swung herself up onto her feet. She began pulling herself
along the hallway, step-by-step. Her legs worked some—
about 50 percent—but it was mostly her shoulders and
arms doing the work. It was probably a good thing she'd
been in such great shape before the accident.

We didn't walk far before she said, "Here we are!" and
we turned to enter a brightly lit room with a bed covered
in a pretty, blue floral bedspread, posters of athletes and
Hemsworth brothers, and all kinds of flowering plants
and books.

"Nice!" I said.

"Yeah, not bad, right? I might even miss having my own
room once I'm done here," Molly chuckled. She crossed to
her dresser, propped herself against it, and took her arms
out of the cuffs of the crutches. She lifted something
from a dish, and palmed it, then in a quick move, she did

a 180-degree turn and I gasped. But she was fine, leaning against the dresser with her back now.

"Don't be a nervous Nellie!" she admonished me. "Now come here. I have something for you to put on. Bud gave this to me as my prize when I was MVP of the lifeguarding squad the summer I was team captain. I think you should have it."

I went and stood with my back to her and Molly lowered a longish necklace over my head.

"Okay, let's see!" she said.

I turned and she smiled and clapped and said, "Look in the mirror."

Above her dresser, I saw my reflection. The necklace was also a silver chain and hanging from the front and center was a tiny silver whistle. It was a lifeguard whistle, but pretty and delicate.

"It's real silver," said Molly. "It works. Try it."

I lifted the whistle to my mouth and blew into it. It gave a shrill *Tweet!* much louder than I had expected, and I jumped in surprise and then laughed. Molly laughed at the expression on my face and gave me a hug.

"Go get 'em, kid!" she said.

DON'T MISS THE NEXT
SUMMER LIFEGUARDS
ADVENTURE!

1

Wake Up!

"Selena! Time to wake up, mi amor!"

My mamí waltzed into my room, snapped up the shades, and flicked on the overhead light. Despite the contrast between her morning-person energy and my night-owl sleepiness, the day started out friendly enough, even though I'd stayed up way too late watching movies on TV while texting my BFs.

"Mamí, it's vacation, remember? I get to sleep late today!" I grumbled. Then I rolled over and tugged the covers over everything but my ear, because I was hoping to hear profuse apologies and the sound of the shades rolling back down.

But who was I kidding? Apologies and rolled-down shades might have come from someone else's mom, but not mine. (Note to self: buy one of those eye-masks like the old-time movie stars wore.)

My mamí moved around my room, efficiently snapping shut the tubes of beauty products on my dresser, rattling the hangers as she re-hung clothes in my closet, and dropping my pens into my pen cup with a sharp tap, tap, tap! It was a symphony of "Wake up!" noises with a melody of "You're messy!" floating on top like an accusation.

"Selena, come! There's no time for late sleeping today. We have only a little while this morning to get organized before I have to work. Get up, get up! And ay, this room! It's a pigsty! It's hurting my eyes!"

I like things a little messy because it makes my room feel cozy and lived in, while my parents' room is so clean,

I bet you could perform surgery in there and not need to sterilize it first.

"Mamí, leave it! You don't have to clean all the time. You're not at work yet!"

Uh-oh. Did I just say that out loud? I pulled the pillow over my ear at last, knowing what was coming next.

"Selena Diaz! How can you be so spoiled? I wish I didn't have to clean all the time, especially at home. But do you think you would remember that when you're throwing your things everywhere? No!" And on and on she went.

Whenever my family fights, we fight in English. My mamí and papí are all Spanishy when they're happy—all their endearments and praise filter through the sweet and gentle words of my early childhood in Ecuador. Amor. Tesoro. Milagro. Corazón.

But when they're mad, they're American.

I lifted the pillow off my ear so I could gauge where she was in her rant.

"...and find you a job!"

"A job?" That wasn't part of the usual rant! I ditched my covers and sat upright in my bed. "What do you mean? I already have the Junior Lifeguards thing in the afternoons that Papí's making me do, plus the extra swim class they say I have to take, and I'm getting tutored for math, which I'm dreading. Now I need to get a job too?" One day out of school and this was already the worst summer of my life. And we were in Cape Cod—summer vacation paradise! Ha!

"Yes. Of course," she persisted. "Now that you are thirteen, you can earn a little of your pocket money, no? I got your working papers already from the school, so let's look at the classified ads, because you can't just sit around during your free time this summer like last year. You know, when I was your age..."

"Ugh!" That was all it took. Every time she launched into how hard it was for her growing up in Ecuador, and how easy we American kids had it, I had to escape. I jumped out of bed without even checking my new phone (a reconditioned iPhone I got for my birthday a few weeks ago) and ran into the bathroom to take my shower. Even with the door closed and the water running, I could *still* hear her ranting on, all in English, about how spoiled American kids are, with our Instagram and lattes and the Mashpee Commons mall.

In the hot shower, I rested my head against the tile and took a deep breath. It's not like we asked to move to America.

I still remember when I was really little, back in Ecuador. I'd loved it. We'd lived on a big ranch with all my cousins and aunts and my abuela and abuelo; all the dads were already in the U.S., making money. It was so peaceful and fun; there had always been someone around to braid my hair or slip me sweets or watch the elaborate plays and performances that we'd put on all the time. No one pressured us: there hadn't been all this talk of grades and careers. Everyone had looked like me, and my mom had been softer, more relaxed, more patient. But here...

well. It's all about success and goals. Every night when I go to kiss my mom goodnight, she is either studying for her accounting exam, ironing a mountain of laundry with starch (some ours and some from the big house), or reading a self-improvement book (thinking of more ways to torture me, I'm sure).

I missed the old days. I struck a tragic pose in the shower, and I tried to really pay attention to my posture and how my body felt in that moment of grief. I made sure I'd be able to call on it for some future performance onstage. Then I rinsed out my conditioner and turned off the water.

Dwelling on the past wasn't going to get me anywhere; we weren't going back to Ecuador, at least for the foreseeable future. Anyway, I wasn't even sure I wanted to.

So, for now, I had to get into character. Acting was what I loved and what I used to tackle life's dramas: in tough moments, I'd create a role in my mind and play it out.

Who knows? Maybe someday my acting skills would

win me an Oscar, and I could go back and buy my *own* ranch in Ecuador!

∽

Costuming is very important in acting. Today I had decided to play the role of "responsible American teenage job-seeker" to calm my mamí down a little. I slid into my seat at the breakfast table wearing a nice pair of long, plaid Bermuda shorts and a cute pink polo shirt with scalloped sleeves. I am pretty short, but well-proportioned, so I am choosy about what I wear and how well it fits me; my mom does a lot of alterations for me by hand.

My papí was running out to a job site, so he planted a kiss on my head and grabbed a cup of espresso my mother had brewed for him. "You look muy bonita, mi amor," he said proudly. "Ready for summer."

"Thanks, Papí," I smiled.

My skin is kind of always tan, and I love makeup and

potions, but today I went barefaced and wholesome (which my parents prefer). I have long dark hair that is thick and gets kind of reddish in the sun. I usually put it in rollers and make it huge and wavy, but today I was wearing it very flat and conservative, with a little barrette at the side. My mother looked at me approvingly as she set down my mug of horchata (a kind of Latin Ovaltine she orders online) and handed me the *Cape Cod Times* and a highlighter.

"Selena, what time does Junior Lifeguards start? What do you need for the course? Where do you meet?" She peppered me with questions as she moved around the kitchen; she seemed to be assembling dinner ingredients.

I glanced at the newspaper but my fingers itched to pull out my phone so I could check in on all my feeds and see what my celebs and friends were up to, and let my public know what I was up to, even if it was not much.

Instead, I remained focused and in character. "I don't know yet," I said. And then, "Oh, Mami! Are you making pupusas for us tonight for a treat?"

"No, mi amor. These are for the girls."

Of course. Anything for "the girls." I poured myself some cereal and began eating it grimly while half studying the help wanted ads.

"The girls" are the Frankel sisters, Alessandra and Samantha, ages eleven and thirteen, who live in the mansion on the dunes, a few hundred yards from here. Their parents employ mine, as cook / head housekeeper and landscaper / property manager. The house we live in is the Frankels', too: it's the estate's caretaker's cottage. The Frankels live in London (Mr. Frankel is a rich Israeli business mogul and Mrs. Frankel is a glamorous African news reporter), so when they are not here on the Cape, which is usually fifty weeks of the year, we have the property all to ourselves: the beach access, the pool, the trampoline, and the vegetable and flower gardens are all ours. It's amazing! I like to pretend I'm a movie star and lie on a float in their pool with a cold lemonade.

But this year, the Frankel girls came with their boy

nanny Nigel for the whole summer, and everything is different. I'm losing my free run of the property. I won't be able to have my friends over because who wants to just sit in my tiny bedroom or on our little scrap of yard? And what if we run into Samantha while my friends are here, and she tries to boss me around? It gives me shivers just to think of it.

"And Selena, speaking of the girls, you must be kind to Samantha at your lifeguards training today. She won't know anyone, so you include her, okay?"

"Ha!" I nearly choked on my cereal. *Kind to Samantha? Me?* "Mamí, trust me. She doesn't want to be seen with me, the hired help." It was my mother's brilliant idea for Samantha Frankel to do Junior Lifeguards this summer. I was furious when I found out.

"Selena, for shame saying such things. Think of Eleanor Roosevelt!" scolded my mother. She likes to quote the former first lady, who supposedly said "No one can make you feel inferior without your consent." I only half understand what that means or even how it applies to me. And why should I have to be nice to the Frankels who have everything?

Here's the deal. The Frankel sisters, Samantha and her younger sister, Alessandra, say hi if we run into each other on the property when we're home, like when I dress up to help Mamí serve at their parents' parties or when I'm bringing starched laundry up on hangers on the golf cart in the morning or whatever. They always remember my name (or someone reminds them of it before they get here). It's just that we all know it's like they are the masters and I am their servant, and I only live here through the good graces of their parents and the hard work of mine. But we do not hang out or pal around off the property. Like, in summers past, if we were to see each other in town or at the movies, we would just look away. It's easier. We all understand the rules. I don't want them messing with my life, and they don't need me in theirs.

That's why Samantha didn't acknowledge me at the

Junior Lifeguards tryouts last week. To be honest, I didn't acknowledge her either. I'm sure she thinks I'm beneath her, so she doesn't want to be seen speaking to me, and that works for me. I don't need any social overlap with Samantha Frankel. Only my best friends know my living situation, and I'd rather keep it that way. I like it that people assume I live on Brookfield Lane because I'm rich. When I post pictures of myself floating in the Frankels' pool on a raft, I caption them *#summer* and *#capecod*, not *#employerspool* or *#maidsdaughter*. It's doesn't hurt anyone to let them think it is my house. And if people don't think I'm rich, well, at least I don't want them to think I'm someone's maid. The bottom line is this: the less my path crosses with Samantha Frankel's, the better.

COLLECT ALL THE
SUMMER LIFEGUARDS BOOKS!

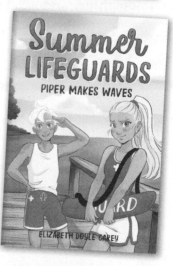

About the Author

Elizabeth Doyle Carey is the author of more than forty books for teens and tweens. A lifelong ocean swimmer, she is scared of big waves and sharks but loves beach glass, dolphins, and whales. Please visit her website at elizabethdoylecarey.com.